Farm Boy

Farm Boy

MARIAN SKEDGELL

A
Joan
Kahn
BOOK

St. Martin's Press
New York

GLOUCESTER LIBRARY

GLOUCESTER, VIRGINIA 23061

Gloucester Library
P.O. Box 2380
Gloucester VA 23061

F
£
SKE

FARM BOY. Copyright © 1985 by Marian Skedgell. All rights reserved. Printed in the United States of America. No part of this book may be used or reproduced in any manner whatsoever without written permission except in the case of brief quotations embodied in critical articles or reviews. For information, address St. Martin's Press, 175 Fifth Avenue, New York, N.Y. 10010.

Design by Laura Hough

Copy Editor: Erika Schmid

Library of Congress Cataloging-in-Publication Data

Skedgell, Marian.
    Farm boy.

    "Joan Kahn book."
    I. Title.
PS3569.K37F3   1985   813'.54   85-25172
ISBN O-312-28295-8

A Joan Kahn Book

First Edition

10 9 8 7 6 5 4 3 2 1

Farm Boy

CHAPTER

1

The man to see, if you want to look at property in High-fields, is Andy McLeod. Andy is eighty-one, but he keeps his hand in.

It's worth calling on Andy just to take his guided tour. In the course of his fifty-odd years selling property in May-wood County, he has given his guided tour to five or ten thousand people, but his enthusiasm for pointing out the celebrity homes and scenic wonders in and around High-fields never flags. He'll take you past the laurel that keeps the southern slope of Hapgood Hill dark green through the winter. He'll take you along Goodfellow Road and Tom's Forge Lane to show you where the famous actors and writers live. He'll point out the glass octagonal house on Pete's Ridge and ask you if you'd like to live there.

And he'll tell you the story of his life. You won't mind because his delight in the telling is contagious. His extraordinary good fortune astonishes him still.

"I was only a farm boy," he'll say. "After school and weekends, I helped out on the Hapgood farm. That was three thousand acres then, only fifteen hundred now. I sold the other fifteen hundred, and sold the farm, too, twice over.

"Mr. Hapgood liked me and fixed it so I would get a scholarship to Cornell if I promised I'd come back and be his manager. Of course I promised. That's a big job to give a young fellow—I was the youngest manager in the county, maybe in the whole state—but Mr. Hapgood had faith in me, he saw I had brains and was honest.

"The long and the short of it is that after I graduated Cornell and was managing the farm no more than a year, Mr. Hapgood dropped dead. Heart attack. So then the estate was tied up the better part of six years. His heirs kept me on as manager. What else could they do? They didn't want to be bothered looking for someone new.

"Now I had a dream, like most young fellows. I didn't want to be working for someone else all my life. I wanted a farm of my own. But how was I, a poor farm boy, ever going to get the money to buy that farm? Good question.

"Then I noticed how much money stuck to the fingers of the lawyers and the real-estate agents when the estate was settled and the farm was sold to the Mayhews. I couldn't be a lawyer, but I could and did get my real-estate license.

"I didn't hit it big right away. Fact is, I had to keep my job on the farm, because in those years we couldn't have lived on what I made from real estate. But I began to make friends with the New York people who were coming up here, and little by little I got established. Came the day I quit working for the Mayhews and a year later I sold the farm for them—in two pieces. Some of the acreage went to a developer—that's where the Blueberry Fields houses are now, but that took ten years. The property went through one developer after another before the houses were actually built. Makes me cry to think of all the money those developers pocketed, selling the land over and over.

"You wouldn't believe, would you, that the first time I sold the Hapgood farm it went for just under three hundred thousand dollars. Three years ago I sold it again, what was left of it, for two and a half million. How's that for a poor farm boy!

"The funny part is, I never did buy that farm I dreamed of when I was young. I could do it easy—I'm a millionaire a couple times over, I don't have to work, you know, I just like getting out and meeting people—but the thing is, farming is hard work. Plain dirty hard work.

"Isn't that a view, there to the south? Those are Wentworth's sheep. Wouldn't that be the ideal spot for a solar home?"

Like Andy McLeod, Dr. Lucille Esker derived a large part of her livelihood from New Yorkers. She hadn't planned it that way. When she went to work for the Maywood Family Clinic, her aim was to escape the big city and its near hysteria about fame. The only child of famous parents, she wished to be through with fame. But as it turned out, she was especially effective in treating the troubled children of famous people. When she succeeded where a host of other psychotherapists had failed with the teenage son of a world-renowned novelist who lived in Highfields, her reputation spread among other celebrities. Instead of sending their adolescents to psychoanalysts on Park Avenue, they sent them to Dr. Esker at the Maywood Clinic.

On this April morning she sat in her office and looked without seeing out the window with its view of a scraggly, untended woodlot. A thin rain fell, further darkening the mat of fallen leaves beneath the still leafless limbs of the trees. Her 10 A.M. patient had just canceled and she had an hour to kill. Not enough time to leave her office to shop, more than enough time to tend to paperwork that Doreen, the clinic's secretary-receptionist, had put on her desk two weeks ago.

Instead she sat there, ruminating on the Academy Awards on television the night before. The public personas of Jack Nicholson (Best Supporting Actor) and Shirley MacLaine (Best Actress) had appeared to her to be seamless with their private selves: Nicholson with that mocking eyebrow—life, fame, the Academy Awards, all of it, a big joke, MacLaine wrestling earnestly in public with the large questions of death and immortality about which she'd just written a best seller—clearly questions she wrestled with in private as well. What was it like to possess a personality so clearly defined that it was like Coca-Cola, a trademark recognized worldwide? What was it like to carry that kind of brand-name persona around with you through all your waking hours? Perhaps it was a little like having to wear the same lettered T-shirt day in and day out, no matter how dirty and stained with perspiration it became.

In the same fashion she'd ruminated countless times about her parents. Her late father had been a symphony-orchestra conductor. Her mother, a retired opera singer, now maintained a studio in Manhattan where she taught aspiring coloraturas. Lucille had no doubt her parents loved her, but they had spent little time with her. She'd been a pleasant-looking little girl, with large hazel eyes and bobbed brown hair. She'd been tidy, punctual, good at taking responsibility—and she still was. Her parents must have found her boring. She found some of her patients boring, which won them an extra measure of sympathy and understanding.

The telephone rang. Doreen said Annemarie Echinger wanted to speak with her. Doreen had never heard of

Annemarie Echinger, but Lucille had. She was a local artist who painted realistic cows against ominous yellow skies. She'd recently been taken up by the New York people.

"Yes, I'm Dr. Esker. May I help you?"

"I'm worried about my daughter and I'd like you to see her. Can you?"

"Is there a chance you could come right over? I've had a cancellation and I'm free until eleven-thirty."

"Well, really, it's not an emergency. I just thought—"

"It's up to you. I'd have to see you first anyway—before I saw your daughter."

"I see."

Lucille could hear her breathing, and somewhere near the phone country music played. "I don't know where you are," Ms. Echinger said.

"In the Maywood Professional Building on Route 502, just past the shopping center."

"All right. I'll be there."

While she waited, Lucille, energized by the prospect of a new patient, tackled the pile of unsigned letters and insurance forms on her desk. She had just signed the last letter when the intercom buzz told her that Ms. Echinger had arrived. She looked up to see a tall woman with a memorable angular face. Her short-cropped fair hair and wind-reddened complexion spoke of time spent outdoors. She wore paint-spattered farmer's overalls over a plaid work shirt.

"I didn't bother to change my clothes," Ms. Echinger said. "Hope you don't mind." Her eyes shifted between the gray couch and the slat-backed chair in front of the old-fashioned desk.

"Not at all. We're pretty informal around here." Lucille motioned her to the chair and poised her pen over a lined yellow notepad. "What's your daughter's name?"

"Allison Friely." Without being asked, the mother spelled out the name. "Friely was my first husband. When we divorced I took back my maiden name. Three years ago I married Marty Grunewald. You know the Grunewald farm?"

"I buy corn there. But you stopped selling eggs."

"It didn't pay."

"How old is Allison?"

"Seventeen. She's a senior at Maywood High."

"Any brothers or sisters?"

"No. She's an only child." The mother spoke bluntly, without inflection.

"What is it about Allison that worries you?"

"She hasn't been acting like herself."

"Exactly how?"

"She's always been active in school affairs and always had lots of friends, full of energy and always on the go. She never went through that adolescent rebellion you read about. And she's very pretty—that's not just her mother talking; everybody says so. But not dumb. She's going to be salutatorian. She's a lot smarter in school than I ever was. I only had one good subject—art."

"Has Allison ever seen a psychologist?" Lucille rose from her desk chair and sat on the couch. Conversation flowed more freely when she sat a few inches below the person sitting in the chair.

"No, never. She's never given me any trouble. I almost went to a shrink after my divorce, but I managed to work it out by myself."

The mother seemed more eager to talk about herself than her daughter. "You started to say that Allison would be salutatorian. Are you worried about her neglecting her studies? A lot of seniors do that in the last semester before graduation."

"No, her grades are just the same. She goes to school every day. She's never sick, always has a perfect attendance record." A wry smile creased Ms. Echinger's leathery face. "You think Allison sounds too good to be true? But she's always been that way, since she was a little girl. Not a troublemaker like I was."

Lucille had heard similar accounts hundreds of times—the well-behaved child who undergoes the classic adolescent rebellion two or three years late. "What is she doing, then, that worries you?"

"Nothing. That's just it. She's not doing anything. If she was starting to run wild, rebelling against me, I'd understand it. I did that to my own mother. But no, she's not doing anything bad. What she does is come straight home from school, sit in her room and read or study, come downstairs for supper, then back up to her room again. She doesn't go out to see her friends, not even on weekends, and she won't talk to them when they call—though they've more or less stopped calling. She's always pleasant to me and her stepfather, but somehow she seems, well, sad. And then last night she—" The mother hunched her shoulders.

Lucille waited.

"Last night she chopped off her hair. She had long golden hair, halfway down her back. All these years she brushed it and washed it, every day. Beautiful hair. I could never grow mine long. It's too fine. That's why I wear it cut short."

"Maybe she was tired of long hair," Lucille said.

"She didn't give it any style. She just hacked it off. As if she was trying to make herself look ugly. She didn't do it to look like me, she did it—I don't know why she did it. That's why I'm here."

"You're right to be concerned. Has Allison ever threatened suicide?"

"Never! I've asked her over and over what's bothering her. All she says is 'Nothing' and walks away."

"How old was Allison when you divorced her father?"

"Only three."

"How did she take it?"

"All right. He came to see her up until she was eleven, when he remarried and moved to California. She's only seen him once since then. He didn't mean that much to her."

"So you two were alone together for a number of years. Was Allison upset when you remarried?"

"She was all for it. She and Marty are a mutual-admiration society. He doesn't have any kids of his own, you know, but he's a really good man. He's given us security we never had before. He thinks my painting is wonderful."

Lucille looked up from her notepad. "I loved that small painting of a red fox you had in the last Maywood Art Association show."

"It sold to a New York City man, Mr. Abramson. He's trying to get me into a gallery there."

"How does Allison feel about your success as an artist?"

Again the brief smile. "She's my biggest booster."

"Do you know of any reason why she should be depressed?"

The mother looked down at her raw-knuckled hands and scraped at a hangnail on her thumb. "I don't know—" Her rather small pale green eyes, fringed by colorless lashes, focused on a spot outside the window. "No—I can't think of a thing."

Lucille noted the mother's hesitation. "Does Allison have a boyfriend?"

"Not a steady. She's always had lots of boyfriends,

smart boys from good families, going to college. But she's never settled on just one."

"Is Allison going to college in the fall?"

"Yes, the University of Wisconsin. She wants to get out of New England, see what the rest of the country is like. And I have some family living around there."

"She might be feeling frightened about leaving Highfields. That's a huge campus." Though Lucille cautioned herself against prejudgment, she'd seen many adolescents whose unacknowledged fear of leaving home and going to live in dormitories—institutions, really—with hordes of strangers, led them into depression.

"We visited there last summer and she said it didn't scare her. She said she was looking forward to it."

Lucille glanced at the clock over the door and went to her desk to look at her appointment calendar. "Do you think you'll have any trouble getting Allison to come to see me?"

"She'll come if I tell her to," the mother said gracelessly. "Whether she'll talk to you is another story."

"That's what we're here to deal with. Could she make next Wednesday at three-thirty? She can take the school bus straight from her last class."

"She has her own car." Again the mother's voice was blunt, uninflected.

Usually, at the end of the interview, the parent expressed gratitude that Dr. Esker was willing to see the troubled child. But Ms. Echinger appeared not to be much given to conventional displays of appreciation. "That's even better. I'll see her Wednesday then." Lucille escorted the mother to the door and, when she had gone, gave Doreen the necessary information for her records.

———

9

Lucille seldom researched a new patient, preferring to form her judgments on the basis of the patient's own words and reactions. But while doing her weekly shopping Saturday afternoon at the Maywood supermarket, she ran into Mavis Sprague, head of guidance at Maywood High.

Mavis was standing midway in the crackers-and-cookies aisle. "Have you noticed anything unusual lately about Allison Friely?" Lucille asked her. "I hear she's one of the stars of the graduating class."

Mavis knew better than to ask the reason for Lucille's inquiry. "She's simply a wonderful young woman. I was only sorry she turned down Yale in favor of one of those big midwestern state universities. But she was determined. She very much follows her own star, though she's not a loner. She's extremely popular."

"And you haven't seen any change in her behavior?"

"Not really." Mavis put a box of soda crackers in her shopping cart. "One thing. She stopped tutoring her cousin—her cousin by her mother's marriage, that is. Billy Durk."

"Colin's brother?"

Mavis nodded.

Last fall, the Juvenile Court judge, feeling uneasy about fifteen-year-old Colin's plea of guilty to killing his father, had asked Lucille to spend some time with Colin before the sentencing. But Lucille had been unable to get the boy to change his story. The Juvenile Court judge had sentenced him to one year at Connecticut Youth Academy. The sentence had six months to go.

"I didn't know Marty Grunewald was related to the Durks."

"Mrs. Durk is Marty's sister."

"Is Billy in Allison's class?"

"Yes, but he might not graduate. He flunked Spanish and needs the credit. I suggested Allison tutor him because he lives next door. He's not stupid. In fact, in some ways he's too smart for his own good. I don't really know why Allison suddenly dropped him, but I can guess."

Lucille had seen Colin's older brother only once—the day in court when he testified that he had tried to wrest the gun from Colin's hands and had been unsuccessful. She'd been struck by his appearance. He was handsome in the brooding way that had made idols of James Dean and Marlon Brando. It was the kind of masculine beauty that carried a latent threat of violence along with vulnerability. Billy's indolent posture on the witness stand seemed to call into question not only the reason for his presence there but the reason for his entire life. "You think he came on to Allison?"

"It wouldn't surprise me. He comes on to every-body—even me." She smiled as she touched her curly gray hair. "He's the sex king of Maywood High. Half the girls have a crush on him, and he doesn't even play football. In fact, he doesn't do anything except exude sex. It's one helluva powerful tool, and he thinks he can use it to rule the world."

"I gather it didn't work on you," Lucille said.

"Nothing to be proud of. He's on the verge of drop-ping out. One of my failures." Mavis shrugged. "If I can do anything for Allison, give me a ring." She wheeled her cart away.

Putting her groceries in her new kitchen cabinets of softly burnished natural oak—partly paid for by the fee she'd received from the state for the hours spent with Colin Durk—she pondered why Annemarie had said nothing about Allison's tutoring. She must have known about it. Billy was her husband's nephew and the Durk farm—what was left of it—bordered on the Grunewald farm. In telling Lucille what had led her to worry about her daughter, perhaps she felt the tutoring was too inconsequential to be worth mentioning.

Allison paused in the doorway.

"Please come in," Lucille said, and motioned to the chair.

The young woman crossed the room with the fluid stride of a fashion model. She was tall like her mother. Her short hair, curled and waved in the latest style, was a darker gold than her mother's, and the face it framed was less angular and unquestionably beautiful by conventional standards. She wore well-tailored slacks rather than jeans, and a yellow shirt under a brown tweed hacking jacket.

Seated, she bent slightly forward, as if to inquire why, of all places on earth, she should be sitting in a psychologist's office on this sunny spring afternoon. Lucille noted no signs of tension in her body.

"I'm sure you wonder why you're here," Lucille said. "Has your mother told you why she was worried about you?"

Allison looked down at her hands loosely crossed in her lap. "Because I cut my hair." A mocking half-smile flicked on and off. "I'm afraid I failed to appreciate the emotional investment my mother had in my long hair."

The reply sounded rehearsed. Allison had had a week to work it up. "Do you honestly believe that's the reason—cutting your hair?"

"What else—" Allison began, then stopped. Her fingers curled into her palms. "Annemarie just doesn't listen. I've told her a dozen times at least that I need some time to myself before graduation. I need time to get to know myself—before it's too late. I'm not the person everyone thinks I am. I know that much."

"What kind of person does everyone think you are?"

"I—" Allison paused. "It would sound like bragging."

"You don't have to worry about sounding immodest here. We're after the truth."

"I don't know the truth. That's what I've been trying to find out."

The girl's hands seemed relaxed again. Allison's retreat into the abstraction called truth was a diversion. "But you do have an idea, don't you, of the impression you make on other people? A good impression, I assume, since you said it would sound like bragging. How is it a good impression?"

"Just that—everybody thinks I've got it all together, I've got all the answers. And that I'm super-straight. I never do anything wrong."

"Do you?"

"Of course. Nobody's perfect."

"But you give an impression of perfection, is that it?"

"That sounds stupid, but—yes." Her rueful smile provided a disclaimer.

"I don't wonder, then, that you wanted to take some time to be alone and think things over. Maintaining an appearance of perfection is awfully hard work."

"Not if you've been doing it all your life." Allison's wide-eyed look was meant to amuse her.

Lucille laughed, as expected. "Then before we can find out who you really are, we'll have to find out why you thought you had to be perfect."

"That's obvious. I was afraid Annemarie wouldn't love me if I wasn't. I've read about the children of divorced parents. That's a pretty common reaction, isn't it?"

Lucille nodded. "Have you been reading books to find out what it is that's troubling you?"

"I don't think I'm troubled. Curious, that's all. I don't have a single symptom of depression. I eat just the same, I sleep all right, I don't have any trouble concentrating—"

Lucille waved her hand to cut her off. "Thank you. You've saved me the trouble of having to ask all those questions." She smiled.

"I'm sorry. I didn't mean to sound like a know-it-all."

After a moment's silence, Lucille said, "Don't you think perhaps you read these books because you're just as worried about yourself as your mother is?"

"Then you'd have to say, wouldn't you, that anybody who studies psychology must be sick in the head."

"There may be something in that."

"What if I said I don't want to come here?"

"Then you wouldn't. It has to be your decision. I certainly wouldn't want you here if you felt coerced. It's almost impossible to make progress with someone who isn't taking part willingly. The therapeutic process is a cooperative endeavor. But I'm sure you know that too."

"It sounds hard."

"It is. It's only worth it if you're hurting and you want to stop hurting."

"It's up to me?"

"Yes. And not a choice you make to please your mother or because she ordered you to make it."

Allison stood. "Then I don't think you'll see me next week. But I enjoyed talking with you." Her smile was brilliant.

"We'll leave it open, shall we?" Lucille escorted her to the outer door. She noticed a single yellow daffodil blooming in the trashy woodlot.

*   *   *

By Thursday afternoon half the faculty and most of the 126-member senior class at Maywood High knew that Allison Friely had been to see a head doctor. A few even knew the doctor's name.

How Allison's visit to Dr. Esker became known is uncertain. Doreen was not supposed to discuss the clinic's patients with anyone, but perhaps because Allison's appearance was so striking, she had told a friend, who told a friend, et cetera. Or someone may have been passing the Maywood Professional Building and seen Allison's car in the parking lot, or even seen Allison enter the building.

In the faculty lounge Mr. Friedman, who taught advanced algebra, calculus, and trigonometry, said, "If someone like Allison has to see a shrink, we're all done for."

Mrs. Haddon, who taught junior and senior social science and was faculty adviser to the senior class, said, "Something's been bothering her. She's on the organizing committee for the graduation ceremonies, but she hasn't attended a single meeting. And she resigned from the yearbook staff. Very strange."

"You never know what they'll do," said Ms. Evans, biology, referring to the established fact that adolescents were unpredictable.

"You can say that again," said Mr. Friedman.

"But I won't," said Ms. Evans.

Allison's classmates were less surprised. Harold Barnes, the class computer whiz, who had once built up enough courage to ask Allison if he could take her to a movie sometime (she'd said, "Why not?" and her answer had made him so happy he'd never dared to follow it up with a specific invitation to a specific movie), said, "There's a lot more going on there than anybody knows about."

His friend Chuck Simon, who was second best in computers and who had never exchanged even a hello with Allison, said, "Anyone as beautiful as Allison is bound to have an identity crisis. How would you like to be judged solely on your *flesh*? Murder!"

By late Sunday afternoon, the news had spread to the monthly Sunday-afternoon musicale sponsored by the widow of Dr. Bronson Eberle, known in the music world as the virtuoso's physician. The performing musicians were Juilliard students, and the invited audience was rewarded with beautifully played baroque music in the drawing room, followed by canapés and drinks on the glass-enclosed terrace overlooking a rose garden. The rosebushes were sprouting their first new leaves.

Lucille was one of the invited. As she moved onto the terrace, the concluding strains of Schubert's "Trout Quintet" running agreeably through her head, she felt a tap on her shoulder. It was Simon Dennis, the staff psychologist at Connecticut Youth Academy. "I understand you're seeing Allison Friely," he said.

"How in the world—?"

"I got it from Colin's brother Billy. I ran into him at Conyac just before coming here."

"He must have heard it at school. Certainly not from Allison. She's stopped tutoring him. Besides, I'm not sure she'll be seeing me." Lucille was disturbed, not by the unsurprising spread of supposedly confidential information, but by her feelings toward Billy's brother. Her failure to get through to Colin, to find out why he'd been so eager to plead guilty, continued to nag her. "How is Colin? Is there any chance he'll be let out early?"

"He's in good shape. His spell in Conyac doesn't seem to be hurting him. But no, he can't be paroled. His sentence was one year, to be served in full. That doesn't mean he'll be stuck behind walls for the next six months. He's been assigned to the farm. I saw him out there just this past week."

"That sounds encouraging. Somehow the thought of him being locked inside was the worst part of the whole ugly scenario. Colin is so in love with the outdoors and all living things, I still can't see him as capable of hurting anyone, let alone his poor drunken father. Well, maybe for once the bureaucracy has managed to do something right."

"Yes," Simon said. "Every now and again, by mistake, we actually end up helping these vicious little animals."

At three-twenty Wednesday, having finished with her two-thirty patient, Lucille closed her eyes and went through a prescribed routine of muscle relaxation. Wilhelm Reich, along with Asian gurus, had promoted the notion that the mind-muscle connection was a two-way street. Somehow when you deliberately relaxed your muscles, your brain also appeared to relax or slow down. The routine worked for her, but over the years she had offered it as a suggestion to less than a dozen patients.

In a corner of her consciousness she had prepared for Allison to be a no-show. Then, as if from a greater distance than she knew to be the case, she heard the outer door in the reception room open and close. She opened her eyes in time to see Doreen showing Allison into her office. Lucille came around her desk. "I'm so glad you decided to come."

Allison stood uncertainly.

"Please sit on the couch. It's more comfortable." Lucille sat on the couch beside her. "Did something in particular happen to help you decide?"

"No." Allison was pale, and there was a hint of listlessness that had been totally absent the week before.

"Did you feel coerced to come here? You look a little beaten down."

"I guess I do."

She's going to make me earn my pay, Lucille thought. "But nobody forced you to come here, did they? Actually, you don't seem to be the kind of person who could be forced to do something against her will."

Allison narrowed her pale green eyes. "That's what you think."

The girl's eyelashes and eyebrows lacked mascara, which accounted in part for her pallor. "You mean that someone has forced you to see me? How? By some kind of threat of punishment? Or were you promised a reward?"

"I was threatened with Annemarie's loss of inspiration." Her voice was flat, like her mother's.

"Does that bother you—that your mother might be unable to paint because she's so worried about you?"

"Of course. So few people are given such a gift, it's criminal not to exercise it to the utmost." Again, Allison sounded as if she were quoting. "Besides, she's on the verge of getting a New York gallery."

"That's an important sign of recognition, isn't it?"

"The most important—next to getting into the big museums like the Met and the Museum of Modern Art."

"Did you ever doubt your mother would achieve that kind of recognition?"

"No. Never!"

The vehemence of her reply signaled that the subject was painful. Allison must often have wondered if the sacrifices she made to please her mother—her steadiness, her goodness, her willingness to accede to whatever demands her mother made of her—were justified. But the doubts had to be repressed. She couldn't allow herself to admit them.

"Well, let's skip what it was that made you come here today, and concentrate on you." She answered Allison's questioning look with a smile. "I'd like to hear again why you decided to drop all your school activities and stop seeing your friends."

"I needed time to be alone and think things over."

"But that implies a problem, doesn't it? Some question you had that neither your teachers nor your friends could answer?"

"Not necessarily. I don't have any problems."

"Could you list for me those activities you decided to give up?"

"German club, drama club, yearbook, senior-class committee, graduation-ceremonies committee . . ." She tapped her chin. "Also I turned down an invite to the senior prom from Walt Haversham, the class president."

To reject an invitation from the class president was noteworthy, but Lucille was more interested in Allison's omission of her tutoring from her list of discontinued activities. "Anything else? Any church or community activities?"

"We don't go to church."

"What about your stepfather's nephews? The older boy is in your class at school, isn't he?"

"Yes."

"That was a terrible tragedy."

"I suppose you could say that." Noncommittal, expressionless.

"Do you ever see the older boy—Billy?"

"No."

"I understand from Mrs. Sprague that he might not graduate."

Allison shrugged.

"Don't you talk about it at home? With your step-father?"

"No."

The stone wall was impressive. Lucille decided to abandon her efforts to scale it. "What about your father? Do you hear from him now that he's moved to the West Coast?"

"He sends me gifts for Christmas and my birthday. I think his wife buys them."

"Before he remarried and moved away, did you see him often?"

"When I was little and we lived in the city, he used to come every Sunday and take me places—the zoo or a museum or a movie. Sometimes when he had the money we'd go to a fancy restaurant where he'd try to teach me the finer points of etiquette."

"How old were you then?"

"Nine or ten. The next year he met my stepmother and I've only seen him once since then—when he came to New York on business."

"Those must have been difficult years for you—just on the threshold of puberty and suddenly losing your father."

"It didn't bother me. I was too busy at school—over-achieving." Her smile was engagingly self-mocking, a deft cover-up for real pain.

Lucille shifted gears once more. "What does Anne-marie think about your stepmother? Is she jealous?"

"What an idea! My stepmother is a simpering little mouse who thinks all men are gods. Dad is her fourth husband."

Significantly, the stepmother remained nameless. "Does your mother ever talk about what caused the divorce?"

"It's no secret. They had different values. Dad wanted

money, Annemarie wanted to be a serious artist. They met while they were students at the Art Institute in Chicago."

"And your father became a commercial artist?"

"He's the art director of a big ad agency in San Francisco." She spoke with a measure of pride.

"Your mother grew up on a farm?"

"A dairy farm in Wisconsin."

"So marrying Marty Grunewald was in a way a return to her roots, wasn't it?"

Allison frowned. "That's only part of it. The divorce was very hard on her."

"Harder than it was on you?"

"Oh, much." The girl gave her a shrewd sidelong look. "You're divorced, aren't you?"

"Yes." Briefly she pictured her ex-husband in his state trooper's uniform.

"Am I allowed to ask why?"

Lucille smiled. "Just this once. I married Lieutenant Littlejohn for the wrong reasons." Her frantic embrace of conventionality, for one. What could be more conventional than marrying a policeman? "We're still good friends."

"Hmm." Allison nodded, as if to confirm a prior observation. "Annemarie married Dad for the wrong reasons, too. She wanted to be citified, sophisticated." Allison flung her arms wide. "Why does everybody want to be what they're not?"

"Do you?" Lucille asked.

"Sometimes."

"Just how would you like to change yourself?"

The girl remained silent. The question was too pointed, too close to what was troubling her.

"Let's leave that for another time," Lucille said, and rose from the couch. "Next week?"

21

"I guess so." As Allison opened the door she smiled fleetingly.

Allison's question echoed in Lucille's mind. Why, indeed did so many people want to be other than they were? Conventional psychology held that such a desire signified self-hatred or an anxiety about whether anybody could love you the way you were. In Allison, as with Lucille herself, the conventional interpretation might apply, but as an explanation it was incomplete. Lucille suspected that Allison felt her mother "loved" her career as an artist more than she loved Allison, just as Lucille had long felt that her parents were more devoted to their musical careers than they were to their child. With maturity Lucille had come to understand that she was confusing two different kinds of love. Eventually she hoped to elicit the same insight from Allison.

Then, too, some adolescents experimented with other life-styles out of a sense of play and curiosity, like the two-year-old who climbs a bookcase to reach the forbidden objects on top. What, after all, had she herself found so inviting in the conventional, the humdrum? It was its otherness, its capacity to surprise her. Long after she had ceased to doubt her parents' love for her or her worthiness of their love, she continued to be attracted by people who symbolized for her middle-class, mainstream America. And Dave had fallen in love with her, she was sure, because to him she also represented the exotic. He was determined not to be a conventional cop. He liked to read poetry, listen to classical music from Telemann to Wuorinen. He took a variety of graduate courses (he had twice the credits he needed for a Ph.D. but was unable to decide on a topic for his dissertation). She had failed him because she wanted him to be what he symbolized for her, not what he was or wanted to be.

They had dinner together once or twice a month. No matter where they dined, someone from Highfields was sure to be there and Dave would hear about it the next day from the troopers at the barracks. Their favorite tack, blunted by repetition, was to warn Dave that he'd end up remarrying Lucille if he didn't watch out. Dave ignored their kidding. Troop B didn't understand why Dave and Lucille had divorced and they didn't understand the situation now. The fact was, as long as he and Lucille lived apart and as long as they avoided sensitive subjects when they met, they enjoyed each other's company. That's as far as it went.

At the Peaceable Kingdom restaurant they sat in their favorite spot overlooking a hillside brook—now nearing flood stage because of unusually heavy April rains. At a bend in the stream the rapid current spun the waterwheel like a top.

"I hear you're seeing Marty Grunewald's stepdaughter," he said as he forked a snail. Lucille had introduced him to escargots, and now, whenever they were on the menu, he ordered them.

"The word does get around," she said.

"I had a little excitement over in that direction a couple of weeks ago." His dark-yellow hair, broad sunburned face, and upslanted blue eyes came from his Polish mother. Years before Dave was born, a schoolteacher whose mission in life was to obliterate ethnicity had changed his father's surname from Gianelli to Littlejohn. "Billy Durk and his girlfriend took off at Easter vacation without telling anybody where they were going. Old man McLeod wanted me to send out a posse."

"What's the connection between Billy and Andy McLeod?"

"The girlfriend is Sally McLeod, Andy's granddaughter.

She lives with the McLeods." Seeing Lucille's questioning look, he added, "Sally's parents were killed in a car crash—three or four years ago."

"I'd forgotten. What did you do?"

"Nothing. They're both of age. McLeod thought they'd run off and got married. Billy was itching to get next to the McLeod millions, he said, but he was wrong." Dave grimaced. The state troopers spent a disproportionate amount of time calming the fears of Maywood County's elderly rich. "Anyway, they're both back home now. Turns out they were invited to spend Easter week at a big estate in the Florida Keys, and they were having such a good time, they just stayed on."

"How would Billy know anybody who owns an estate in Florida?"

"Met him at Garrison Craig's."

"The movie director?"

"So-called." The skeptical grin looked out of place on Dave's open country-boy face. "The guy with the estate made a killing in computers and is backing a movie Craig is going to direct. Someone named Farnol. I checked him out. He's legit."

"I thought Craig hadn't directed a movie since the 1940s. And they were only B or C movies even then."

"What can I say?" Dave spread his big hands. The gesture was something he'd copied from television cop shows in his search for big-city sophistication. "Anyway, here's a better story. Did you read about our catching that California embezzler?"

"Who didn't? It was on the front page of *The New York Times*."

"They didn't print the whole story."

"One of your new troopers caught him, wasn't that it?"

"The only rookie I have is Highfields's resident

trooper, Harry Walsh. Harry the Hound we call him now. An amazing kid. He's got a photographic memory. You know what he does in his spare time? He goes over old Wanted posters. The embezzler's mug shot was on a poster three years ago."

"The *Times* said he'd been living here in Maywood all that time."

"Under a new identity. And working for a bank, too. Can you beat it? It was just his bad luck to be sitting across a desk from Harry the Hound when Harry went for a car loan."

"Does Harry get a reward?"

"We're looking into that. The California bank's insurance company ought to give him something. What Connecticut pays resident troopers, the kid could sure use it."

Dave's genuine pleasure at the young trooper's good fortune was one of his most attractive qualities. Why couldn't she appreciate him for what he was?

Something was missing from Dave's story about Billy Durk and Sally McLeod. Over coffee and strawberry tart, she returned to it. "Why didn't Billy's mother call you? Or the high school?"

"From all I can see, the high school figured he'd dropped out. But he's fooled them. He's back in school and your friend Mavis tells me he's going to graduate. Billy may not be school-smart, but he's not dumb."

Lucille wondered if Allison had resumed tutoring Billy. She'd try to find out at their next session. "I still think it was Billy, not Colin, who killed their father. And most of Highfields agrees with me."

"No fingerprint on the trigger." He nodded to the hovering waitress to pour more coffee. "No way to tell for sure."

"It's so easy to see why Colin would plead guilty. He

was sentenced as a juvenile. Billy would have been tried as an adult. I just can't see Colin pointing a gun at anyone."

Dave grumbled—it was an old point of contention between them. "They did it together. Their old man beat their mother once too often. And don't forget the arguments about money. Sam Durk grabbed every dollar the boys earned and dropped it at the Overlook Bar. The way I see it, he drove them to it."

"Colin's fingerprints were on the gun barrel because he grabbed it trying to stop his brother." Seeing Dave's frown, she smiled. "We agree to disagree."

"Everybody's down on Billy, but if you ask me, his bad rep comes mostly from his way with the ladies. In Maywood County there's a lot of repressed sexual jealousy."

"Only in Maywood County?" Their laughter harmonized agreeably. "But why didn't his mother know where he was? I thought he was close to his mother."

"Mae Durk doesn't know where *she* is half the time. You should have seen their place—garbage in the sink, the toilet stopped up—"

"Did you call Health Services?"

"I called her caseworker. They sent over a house cleaner. And a plumber. At least, that's what the caseworker told me."

"But what about Mrs. Durk? Shouldn't she be seeing somebody?"

"Like a therapist, you mean? That's up to her caseworker and Medicaid. Sometimes I think the troopers do more social work than the people hired to do it."

"Colin could be better off at Conyac than he would be at home—much as it troubles me to give good marks to any so-called correctional facility."

Dave grinned and asked for the check. He insisted on paying, not, he said, as a symbol of male superiority but as a token of their friendship and his high regard for her. She had ceased making an issue of it.

Allison dragged her feet across the carpeted floor and sat heavily on the couch. Her pale eyes were red-rimmed and again without mascara.

Lucille sat beside her. "Won't you tell me about it?" she asked.

Allison lifted her head. "It's nothing really. Nothing important."

"It must be important to you if it makes you feel this bad."

"But it's so silly. I know there's nothing I can do about it."

Lucille put her hand over Allison's clenched fist. "About what?"

"Evil. Evil in the world. It's an old theological problem, isn't it?"

"Yes, but it's one each person has to solve, just as we have to solve the problem of pain and suffering. Is there something specific that you consider evil?"

Allison turned away. "Power," she said to the wall. "Power to destroy. To kill."

"Do you know someone with that kind of power?"

Allison nodded.

Lucille made a wild stab. "Tell me about some of your friends at school. Are they affected by this evil power?"

"Some of them."

"Like Sally McLeod?"

Allison looked startled. She said nothing.

Lucille rose and walked toward her desk. "No, I'm not a mind reader," she said with a smile. "I heard from Lieutenant Littlejohn that Sally and Billy Durk had left town for

Easter vacation and had come back only a few days ago. Were you worried about them, or about Sally?"

The words tumbled out compulsively. "She's his slave. She'll do anything he tells her to do. Billy deliberately makes girls do disgusting things so they'll be his slaves. That's what Manson did. Billy's read every book there is about Charles Manson. It's a psychological trick. If you agree to do something awful, you have to worship the person who told you to do it in order to rationalize why you did such an awful thing." The spurt of words seemed to energize her. She opened her purse and took out a pocket mirror. "I look terrible, don't I?"

"Not so bad, considering." Possibly Allison's troubling change in behavior sprang from a need to build a containing wall around moral anarchy. "Did Billy try to enslave you?"

Her eyes were fixed on her fingers twisting in her lap. She nodded.

"Was this while you were tutoring him?"

After a pause Allison nodded again.

"Have you resumed tutoring since he's returned from Florida?"

"No!" She shook her head violently.

"Is Billy the reason you've stayed so close to home recently?"

"I don't want to be in the same room with him—ever!"

"Are you afraid you wouldn't be able to resist his immoral proposals if you were?" She observed Allison make a deliberate effort to appear calm.

"He disgusts me," she said coolly. "I feel—contaminated—when I'm near him. He's completely evil. He killed his father, you know."

"Most of us suspected he did," Lucille said. She concealed her surprise at the turn her inquiry had taken.

"Of course his father was a terrible man," Allison continued. "He used to tie Billy and Colin to the bedpost and beat them with a leather whip."

"I didn't know that."

"That's no excuse for murder, is it?"

"No."

"And now Billy thinks he can get away with—anything."

"Anything?"

"He says the minute Colin gets out of Conyac, he's going to kill him, too." Allison shivered.

Lucille put her arm around the frightened girl. "How long have you known about this?"

"Since winter, February, when I started tutoring him."

"Maybe he was just trying to impress you."

"It wasn't bragging. He means it." Allison raised her pale face. "I can't think of anything I can do. I mean for Sally and for Colin. Before it's too late."

Lucille, as a graduate student, had replicated the classic experiment of the rat placed in an insoluble maze. When the rat discovers there's no egress, no matter what path it takes, it sits motionless in a corner, collapsed into apathy and depression. "But Billy isn't going to kill Sally, is he?" she said. "It sounds to me as if he and Sally had quite a glamorous spring vacation."

"I told you—she's his slave."

"Don't you sometimes think being someone's slave might not be such a bad thing? If you loved him?"

"That's not real love."

"Does Billy attract you? You said you were afraid to be in the same room with him." Allison's characterization of Billy as evil might be a projection onto him of how she viewed her own sexual feelings.

"You'd be afraid of him, too. He's an animal!"

"Some animals are very nice. Your mother is a gifted painter of animals."

Allison glared at her. "Don't play those word games on me. They don't mean anything. Any more than dreams. It's all nonsense."

Lucille ignored the girl's attack. "Speaking of dreams, do you ever dream about Billy—or somebody like him?"

"I don't dream, period."

"Everybody dreams. See if during the coming week you can't remember a dream or two. I'm not a Freudian, but there are messages in dreams. We might be able to find out what really troubles you about Billy Durk."

Allison failed to smile on departing. Anger had displaced the girl's fearfulness—a step in the right direction.

But the session had left Lucille with a problem. Should she tell Dave about Billy's threat to kill his brother? Confidentiality was no excuse when a doctor or lawyer learned of an impending crime and failed to inform the police. She needn't bring Allison into it, but Dave would undoubtedly guess that Allison was the source of the information. Might she be placing Allison in danger? She was convinced that Billy had made the threat only to impress Allison. Evil, or the appearance of evil, was a potent aphrodisiac—a truth the packagers of pop-music stars shrewdly exploited. But on the slim chance the threat was real, she dare not keep silent.

After her final patient of the day, she continued to wrestle with the question as she drove home in her cranky brown Volvo. Oaks were just beginning to leaf out. Yellow forsythia and daffodils brightened the rich new green of lawns. Spring flowering was two weeks late because of the heavy cold rains. The farmers had had to delay their planting. Those who had rushed the season found that their fields turned to mud, seeds and topsoil washed down into lakes and rivers. The unhealthy weather had contributed to widespread flareups of arthritis and mental depression.

She left the Volvo in her driveway and entered the back door of her house, a former guest cottage on the grounds of a large estate that had been sold to real-estate developers. She rang the troopers' barracks and learned that Lieutenant Littlejohn had just left. Since it took Dave a few minutes to drive to his garage apartment in High-fields, she poured herself a glass of sherry and sat at her kitchen table. It always felt good, returning to her little home after a day of work. When she and Dave were divorced, they'd sold their lovely old colonial house, splitting the proceeds. Dave chose not to buy another house because he planned to "move on"—to some grander law-enforcement job in a big city. But Lucille had bought the cottage almost immediately, and remodeling the kitchen and decorating the rest of the house had proved to be good therapy for the pain of the divorce.

She dialed Dave's number. He answered on the second ring.

"I've learned something I think you should know about—in your official capacity," she said.

"Shoot."

"It's about Billy Durk. He's been heard making threats to kill his brother when Colin gets out of Conyac."

"That confirms it then, doesn't it?"

"What do you mean?"

"That he was the one who pulled the trigger. He's afraid when Colin gets out of Conyac he'll tell what really happened."

"It looks that way."

"I'll drop around and have a talk with Billy. I've been meaning to do that anyway."

"You won't mention the threat, will you?"

"For Chrissakes, Lucille, will you stop treating me like I'm retarded!"

"Sorry."

"Thanks for being a good citizen."

"You're very welcome."

Lieutenant Littlejohn drove slowly along West Road, which bordered what had once been the Durk farm. Billy's father had sold most of it to real-estate developers. The land had been resold again and again, at ever increasing prices, but no homes had been built on the property as yet. Billy's uncle, Marty Grunewald, whose 200-acre dairy farm adjoined the property on the south, rented the land from the developers, planting corn and soybeans.

The furrowed fields looked newly plowed. There was standing water in several low spots.

Twenty years ago, when Sam Durk had moved in with his bride, Mae Grunewald, he had sheathed the tall, narrow farmhouse in white asphalt shingles. The shingles were now a dirty gray, chipped and broken. Some were missing. Window frames and the sagging side porch were barren of paint. The wood was cracked and rotting.

Seeing the Durk farmhouse always gave Dave a heavy feeling in his chest. He had grown up on the same kind of broken-down farm in northeastern Connecticut. His father constantly experimented with the latest farming methods, only to abandon them halfway through out of laziness or boredom. Dave's mother wept and went to church. By the time Dave was in his teens, he understood that anything that needed doing he would have to do himself. He saw nothing idyllic or picturesque about farming. Unlike the visitors from New York, he knew of the ugly rural slums hidden in the deep valleys and on the rocky slopes of scenic hills.

Education was his way out. The United States government, via the Army, paid for his undergraduate education. The state of Connecticut paid for his graduate studies.

From the road Dave could see and hear Billy. On the hard-packed dirt between house and barn, Billy was circling on a brand-new Yamaha. Its chrome blinded in the intermittent sunlight. Sally McLeod sat on a tree stump in front of the open barn door. When she saw Dave approaching, she waved and said, "Hi, Lieutenant."

Billy gunned the engine, then roared to a halt. A blue exhaust cloud hung in the air.

"That's some bike," Dave said. "Where'd you get it?"

"I'm trying it out." Billy's cocky grin challenged Dave to make something of it. "I might decide to buy it."

"Pretty expensive, isn't it?"

"Five grand." Billy winked at Sally. "I've got a nice piece of change coming in." His grin widened. "Perfectly legal, Lieutenant. I won't mess with nothing shady."

"When you buy it you'll have to keep an eye out for Welfare," Dave said. He looked at Sally. Tight jeans and a V-necked pink sweater set off her small shapely body. Her total absorption in Billy gave some definition to her pretty childlike face, but the purple eye shadow and bright pink lipstick looked cheaply theatrical, and the yellow curls cascading down her back must have taken hours to accomplish.

"Welfare takes care of Ma. They don't take care of me," Billy said.

"You both back in school after your vacation?"

"Yes, we are," Sally said. "And we're both going to graduate. I'm helping Billy with his Spanish."

"Is that what Allison was tutoring you for?" he asked Billy.

"Yeah, but Sally's a better teacher." He leered at Sally.

Her lips framed a kiss. "I learn a lot faster from Sally than I ever did from Allison."

"That's good to hear." Dave paused. "How's your brother getting along? He's got, what? Six months to go at Conyac?"

"About that." Billy looked unconcerned. "They got him working on the farm. Slave labor," he added with his irritating grin.

"Do you worry about his getting out?"

Billy shrugged. "Why should I worry? I won't be around. I'm splitting Hicksville the day I get my piece of paper."

"Any idea where you plan to go?"

"I'm working on it. Sally wants to go with me—I don't know why." Billy widened his eyes in mock wonder. "She says she'd just run away from that girls' college her rich grandpa wants to send her to. But I think she should do what her grandpa wants her to do, don't you, Lieutenant?"

The urge to get his fingers around Billy's throat was so strong, Dave thrust his hands into the pockets of his windbreaker. "Andy McLeod usually gets what he wants," he said. "I'm glad you're both planning to graduate. Good luck."

As he walked toward his car, he heard them both giggling and then the sound of the Yamaha revving up.

CHAPTER

2

About halfway through their session, Lucille asked, "Do you have any dreams to report?"

"Not a dream really. You know the time when you're lying in bed in the morning, and you're not quite awake and your mind wanders? That's when I had this dream or vision or whatever you want to call it." Allison was beginning to warm toward Lucille. Her suspicion and defensiveness diminished with each session.

"What morning was it?"

"Just this morning. My subconscious must have reminded me that you asked me to bring in a dream, and this morning was my last chance to follow instructions. I always follow instructions."

Lucille ignored the bait. "Can you describe it?"

"It wasn't much. I mean nothing much happened. I was standing at the mouth of a tunnel—a long dark tunnel, not as big as a highway tunnel like the Lincoln Tunnel into New York. More like the tunnel the train goes through coming into Grand Central."

"But you were standing outside it."

"Yes. On one side and looking into it, because it sounded like someone was calling to me from far inside. It sounded like 'Allison, Allison,' but hollow and echoing. It wasn't clear. It could have been just the sound of wind in the tunnel. And I was terrified to take even one step into the tunnel. I just stood there and listened."

"Was it a man's or a woman's voice?"

Allison frowned. "I couldn't really tell because of the echo. It could have been a woman's voice or a boy's."

"Did it sound like the voice of anyone you know?"

"No, it didn't."

"And that's all there was to your dream?"

"Yes. I just stood there listening to the sound and not moving—until I finally woke up."

"You felt afraid."

"More than that. I was paralyzed. I don't know why."

"Maybe we'll find out one day." In classic Freudian dream interpretation a tunnel is a symbol for the womb. The dream confirmed that repression of her sexuality might be one source of Allison's depression. "May I ask you an intimate question? You don't have to answer it if you don't want to." Lucille paused. Allison looked merely curious. "Are you a virgin?"

"No."

"Was your first experience of intercourse a good one?"

"No."

"You didn't enjoy it?"

"No."

The blunt answers were disturbing. "Have your subsequent experiences been enjoyable?"

Allison turned her eyes toward the wall. "I haven't had any subsequent experiences," she said in a voice so low it was barely audible.

"Does that worry you?"

"No."

"Was your first and only experience traumatic in any way?"

"I was raped." The words were delivered without emotion.

"I see." Rape and subsequent celibacy were all too common. "How old were you?"

"Fourteen. Three years ago. When we first came here—to Highfields."

"Did you tell your mother?"

"No. I didn't want to upset Annemarie. She and Marty were so happy."

"You didn't tell anybody? You've kept it a secret all this time?"

Allison nodded.

"Do I know the person who raped you?"

Again Allison nodded and faced the wall.

"Was it Billy Durk?"

"Yes."

Why had the girl ever agreed to be his tutor, to sit alone with him in a room, going over Spanish vocabulary while she buried her memory of pain and violation? The pressure on her not to worry her mother must have been overwhelming. Little wonder Allison had chosen seclusion as the only safe escape route.

"Rape victims often have very ambiguous feelings about their attacker. Some even fall in love with him."

"That's sick!"

"What I'm trying to tell you," Lucille continued, "is that if Billy came on to you while you were tutoring him, and you responded, that is, if he aroused you, it's not something you need to be ashamed of, it's not unnatural." The girl's stiffened posture worried her. Perhaps Lucille had led her too far too fast. "Well, let's come back to this another time. I'd like to hear more about those years when you and Annemarie were alone together—after the divorce."

Allison's posture eased. "We really were pretty happy. Annemarie designed greeting cards. Whenever one of her designs was accepted, we had a big celebration. I went to nursery school and then P.S. 41. I saw Dad almost every Sunday. Most of the kids I knew had divorced parents, so I didn't feel strange or different. I didn't feel deprived. I just felt—normal and happy."

Lucille nodded at this glossy, retouched portrait of Allison's childhood. She chose not to question it since Allison needed it to bury the ugly memories that Lucille had unwittingly forced her to disinter.

Dave was almost out the door, on his way to his Saturday morning Russian class at the University of Connecticut, when he heard his phone ring and turned back. It was Trooper Walsh.

"I didn't know whether I should bother you or not," Harry said. "I just got a hysterical call from Mr. McLeod's granddaughter. She says her boyfriend is missing."

"For how long?"

"She says she was supposed to have a date with him last night, but he never showed. She was so worried she didn't sleep all night and called his home around an hour ago, about seven A.M. His mother told her he wasn't there. She went into his bedroom to look and the bed was still made up, so he probably wasn't home all night. Anyway, I thought I should call you. I told the girl it was still too early to put out a missing person's."

"Was Sally very upset?"

"I told you—she sounded hysterical. She said he had

this brand-new motorcycle and she was sure he'd got into an accident somewhere."

"Check the hospitals and police reports, just in case. I'll call in this afternoon. I talked to Sally and Billy early this week and saw the bike. He was trying it out. He must have got the money to buy it and took off."

At 1 P.M. Dave returned from his three-hour intensive course in Russian (he wanted to be able to read Russian law-enforcement literature in the original; perhaps he would do his dissertation on law enforcement in a Communist country). He phoned the barracks.

"Any news about Billy Durk?"

"No. Nothing on the wires either. The girl, Sally, called twice. She's positive something has happened to him."

"When was the last time she saw him?"

"Yesterday afternoon. She works in her grandpa's real-estate office in Highfields on Friday afternoons, and Billy came by on the bike. He said he just bought it. You were right about that."

"He must have got the money he was expecting. I'd sure like to know what he had to do to get that kind of money." Dave paused. It was still too early to send out a missing person's. Besides, the kid could be anywhere, roaring along the twisty roads, enjoying himself. He might have spent the night at a friend's house. "Did Sally say she'd called Billy's friends?"

"Every one of them. Nobody's seen him since yesterday."

"Call the Yamaha dealer. Find out what the transaction was with the bike. I can't believe Billy had it all in cash. He must have had to sign something, wait for a check to clear, something like that. See what you can find out and call me back. I'll be here all afternoon—studying."

"Will do."

Dave found himself unable to concentrate on his studies. Russian was easy for him because of its similarity to Polish, which his mother spoke at her family's gatherings. His relatives loathed the Russians and couldn't understand why he wanted to learn the detested language. "It's better to know the enemy," he said.

But he couldn't keep his mind on the exercises. The question of Billy's money teased him. Billy had made a point of telling Dave the money was "legal," so it couldn't be drugs. If Billy had been delivering contraband (cigarettes, whiskey, girlie magazines) to Conyac, he wouldn't get that much money in a lump. Besides, contraband at Conyac was tightly controlled by the big-city kids from Bridgeport and Hartford. They discouraged competition.

So where and for what did Billy get it?

The phone rang.

"You had the right idea," Harry said. "The Yamaha dealer says Durk only put a down payment on the bike and the dealer wasn't going to transfer title until the check cleared. But to do the kid a favor, he lent him the bike for the afternoon. Now he's climbing the walls because the bike wasn't returned. He's called the bike clubs—they go on weekend outings all around here—and they're on the lookout for a Yamaha FZ-750. If it's anywhere within two hundred miles, they'll find it. What the hell, the kid would at least have to stop for gas somewhere."

"Did the dealer tell you what the down payment was?"

"One grand. Where'd a Durk kid get that kind of money?"

"And how was he going to pay off the rest of it? That's a five-thousand-dollar bike."

"I don't think it's drugs," Harry said. "I have a pretty good idea who the dealers are up at Maywood High."

"I thought the same thing. Well, he'll probably come wandering home before the weekend's over. If he doesn't, we'll put out a missing person's on Monday."

By Sunday night it was clear that Billy and the bike had vanished. The bikers had checked at gas stations along all the main routes out of the county, and none reported seeing the brand-new Yamaha at their pumps. Late Sunday night Dave called Mrs. Durk.

"Are you sure you haven't heard from Billy since Friday?" he asked her.

"He's a good boy. He's all right," she answered.

"But have you heard from him? Have you talked with him on the phone?"

"Why would he call? I told you he's all right."

"We don't think he's all right, Mrs. Durk," Dave said. "We're afraid something has happened to him. Please call us the minute you hear from him." Dave gave her the phone number of the barracks and double-checked that she had written it down.

On Monday morning the missing person's report was distributed, accompanied by a photograph of Billy that Harry found in the Durk murder-case file. Dave stopped at the small Highfields branch of the Maywood Bank and confirmed that Billy had deposited a check for a thousand dollars around two-thirty on Friday. The check was in the process of being cleared. Helen Wadsworth, the only full-time teller at the Highfields branch, had handled the transaction.

"I remember it because you have to wonder where Billy would get that much money," she told Dave. "It was a company check—a company called Education Services or something like that. Like one of those companies that get the kids to sell magazine subscriptions. Except that I don't think you could make a thousand dollars selling magazine subscriptions."

"Do you remember the company's address or the address of the bank the check was drawn on?"

"No. I'm sorry."

"How can I find out?"

"You'd have to trace the check through the computer, and you'd need a court order, wouldn't you? Unless, of course, the check bounces." She smiled uncertainly.

"If Billy doesn't turn up in a couple of days, I'll be back," Dave said. "Or let me know if the check bounces."

He spent the rest of the morning at the barracks answering phone calls from newspaper reporters. He got calls from the three New York City newspapers as well as the five local newspapers.

The morning was also punctuated by calls from Sally McLeod. She was too upset to go to school. "You'll let me know the minute, the very minute you hear anything? Please," she said.

"Of course. Maybe you could help us. Will you be home all afternoon?"

"I'm not leaving the phone."

"I'll be around."

After lunch he drove to the McLeods' Windrush Farm—a farm in name only. The large colonial-style house fronted on a circular driveway. The professionally landscaped grounds were meticulous. Behind the house were a large swimming pool and cabana. Opposite the house's west wing was a tennis court.

This, Dave thought, is what money can buy. He paused for a moment in admiration. Windrush Farm looked especially beautiful after the bountiful spring rains. Rose, pink, and white azaleas bordering the driveway were in full bloom, the blossoms mottled by sunlight that filtered through towering oaks and spruces.

Rose McLeod was standing at the front door as he drove up. She was almost as tall as her husband, large-boned, with a blunt manner and a harsh voice. "Sally's in the sunroom," she said, motioning toward open French doors off the marble-floored foyer. "I don't know why she's carrying on so over that miserable boy. It wouldn't bother me if he never showed up."

On the threshold of the sunroom, Dave paused. Sally was sitting in a wicker armchair, her eyes swollen from weeping. "Is there any news?" she asked.

"Nothing. Sorry." He would have liked to assign Harry or another young trooper to interrogate Sally, but he couldn't in fact spare a single one of them. Each of the small towns in the southeastern quadrant of Maywood County was given a resident trooper responsible for patrolling its roads and answering its citizens' calls. Only the town of Maywood was large enough to have its own police department and jail.

"Let's get started," he said, sitting on a wicker couch and taking from his pocket a notepad and pen. "Can you give me the names of Billy's friends—everyone you called and even those you didn't."

Nervously, in a halting childish voice, she named a dozen of Billy's classmates and his co-workers at a trash-removal company that employed him twenty hours a week.

"Anybody else?"

Sally shook her head.

"Tell me again what direction Billy was headed when he left you Friday afternoon."

"He turned left, going east on 502."

"Do any of his friends live in that direction?"

"I don't think so."

"Can you think of anything or anyone he might be going to see in that direction?"

"Only Conyac."

"Maybe he wanted his brother to see his new bike."

"Maybe."

"I'll give Conyac a call." The lead wasn't worth much. Even if Billy had driven over to Conyac to show off his Yamaha 750, where had he gone from there? "Something's been bothering me," he said.

She looked at him with more than curiosity. Was it fear?

"I have to wonder where Billy got the thousand dollars he put down on the bike. And where he planned to get another four thousand. Do you happen to know?"

She shook her head and looked down.

Dave bent toward her. "I think you do know. And it might help us find Billy."

"No, it wouldn't."

"You're sure of that?"

She shifted her gaze. "I promised Billy I wouldn't tell. It isn't anything bad. It isn't."

"Will you tell me in a couple of days—if we still haven't found him?"

She nodded, and began suddenly to sob.

Dave waited while she wiped her tears. "Is there a chance Billy might have headed back to Florida, to where you spent spring vacation?"

"No. Dane and Marge—Mr. and Mrs. Farnol—were on the plane with us, coming back. It's Mr. Farnol's plane. He closes the Florida place April to November. There wouldn't be anybody there."

"Where are the Farnols now?"

"They have an apartment in New York. They might be

there." Her voice remained shaky, but she seemed less apprehensive. "Garrison would know—Mr. Craig."

"Have you talked to Garrison Craig—about Billy?"

"I called Friday night. Garrison wasn't there. He's gone to California."

"About that movie he's directing?"

The uncertain look returned. "I guess so."

"Could Billy have gone with him?"

"Why?"

"Just a thought." And not a very intelligent one. If Billy had taken off in a plane, where had he left the motorcycle? Why hadn't he taken any clothes with him? Or told Sally? "Call me if you think of any names to add to the list," he said, rising.

Back at the barracks he phoned Tom Rolphe, the assistant superintendent at Conyac. After explaining the reason for his call, he asked to speak to Colin Durk.

"Colin's working on the farm," Rolphe said. "I'll have him call you when he comes back in."

"About when will that be?"

"About four."

"Thanks. I'll be here."

Dave put Trooper Phil Corbin to work matching phone numbers and addresses to the names Sally had given Dave. Phil had a partial disability, so he worked inside the barracks as an administrative aide. By the time Phil had completed the chore, it was late enough in the afternoon for Billy's friends to be home. The four-to-midnight shift came on as Dave started phoning them.

Halfway through, the call came in from Colin Durk.

"Colin, did you happen to see your brother last Friday?" Dave asked him.

"No, sir. I was working on the farm."

"When was the last time you saw Billy?"

"He came by a week ago Sunday."

"Did he tell you he was planning to buy a motorcycle?"

"Yes, sir. He said he'd come around as soon as he got it. I was kind of wondering why I didn't see him yesterday."

"Would Billy have known you'd be working on the farm Friday?"

"I think so."

"Would there be any way for him to show you the bike there?"

"Not close up. The farm's a ways in from the road, and there's some pretty thick woods."

"Could you have seen him if he was on the road?"

"Not unless I was over at the north end of the cornfield—that's a kind of high spot where you can see over the woods to the road."

"But you didn't see him."

"No, sir."

"Do you have any idea where he might be?"

"No, sir."

"If you think of anything, you'll call me right away, won't you."

"Yes, sir."

Dave couldn't tell from Colin's voice on the phone whether Colin was worried about his brother or not.

He went back to the list. When he called Billy's employer, the trash-removal service, he got an answering service and left a message for the employer to call him.

He kept at it through dinnertime—Phil brought him in a hamburger and fries, which he gobbled at his desk. Around eight he called New York Information on the slim chance that the Farnols had a listed number. As he suspected, their number was unlisted.

A few minutes later the phone rang and it was Rick Hallberg, Billy's employer. Rick hadn't known Billy was a missing person. "When he didn't show up Saturday, I figured he just took off again," Rick said.

"What days does he work?"

"Mondays, Wednesday afternoons, all day Saturday. Total twenty hours. He's a pretty good worker—when he's there."

"What day do you pay him?"

"Saturday. I kinda wondered why he didn't come by at least to pick up his check."

"So you haven't seen him since Wednesday?"

"That's right."

Although Dave hadn't expected results from the telephone calls, he felt depressed by the lack of payoff for his efforts. The little he'd learned—in particular, Billy's failure to pick up his paycheck—convinced him that Billy had not left the area willingly. Where could he have gone—or been taken? Tracking dogs wouldn't help. Billy had been on a motorcycle, not on foot.

The time had come to appeal to the public. Dave drafted a notice:

Anybody seeing a young male riding a new Yamaha FZ-750 motorcycle in the general area of Route 502 on Friday afternoon, April 20, please call (203) 611-2211 (Highfields Barracks).

He'd get Phil to phone the local newspapers and radio and TV stations first thing in the morning.

CHAPTER

3

The rains returned in full force on Tuesday and continued through Wednesday morning, by which time everybody in Maywood County who listened to the radio or watched TV or read a newspaper knew that Billy Durk was missing.

Dave received three calls offering information on Wednesday. Two were crank calls. The third was from a teacher at Maywood High who was leaving Swifty Dry Cleaners on Route 502 when she saw Billy roar past. Swifty's was about a quarter mile east of McLeod's Highfields office and about one mile west of Conyac.

Dave put in an order for use of a police helicopter and crew on Friday—a week to the day Billy had disappeared. Unless he received information to the contrary, he planned to have the helicopter make an aerial surveillance of the woods and fields on either side of Route 502. The trees hadn't completely leafed out, so the gleaming chrome of a new bike should be easily visible. His main worry was the weather. If it poured on Friday, he'd have to put off the helicopter search until Monday. His budget couldn't take double weekend pay for the helicopter crew.

He alerted Hugo Bannerman, Maywood's police chief, and Rolphe at Conyac that a helicopter search was scheduled for Friday over areas in their jurisdiction. Bannerman insisted he should be aboard the helicopter.

"Leave it to the crew," Dave said. "They know what they're doing. We'll patrol 502 during the search. If you want to come along, be my guest."

"We'll do our own patrol, thank you. If you find Billy Durk in Maywood, it's our business. Right?"

"Right," Dave said.

Because nobody she knew was talking about anything else, Lucille decided to tackle the subject of Billy Durk head-on. "What do you think has happened to him?" she asked Allison.

Allison showed no surprise at the question. "I think somebody's killed him."

"Is that wish fulfillment?" Lucille said with a smile.

"No. Just good sense. Billy's such a show-off, even if he had two broken legs he'd still be wheeling that bike around to make sure everybody saw it."

"And the fact that he isn't means that he's dead?"

"Has to be."

Allison's emotionless tone continued to worry her. Lucille could only surmise the extent of turmoil it masked. But she backed off from questioning Allison about the rape. Examination of that traumatic experience would have to wait until Allison herself volunteered to talk about it.

"You wouldn't be sorry if Billy was dead, would you?"

"I think it's sad for anybody to die, especially so young."

"Do you ever think about being dead?"

"Sure. Who doesn't?"

"Are you afraid of dying?"

"Sometimes. Sometimes I think it would be nice, peaceful—" She spread her arms. "No more problems."

"Tell me about your problems."

The silence lasted for several minutes.

"I don't think I can fall in love," Allison said at last. "Everybody I know has fallen in love, but I can't."

Lucille nodded. "Falling in love is different from loving someone, isn't it?"

"In a way."

"How would you describe the difference?"

Allison nibbled her bottom lip. "Loving someone is quiet, steady. Falling in love is sudden, passionate—"

"Out of control?"

Allison's eyes lit with understanding. "Yes, out of control."

"And you don't like to lose control, do you?" Especially after the ultimate experience in loss of control over one's own person, which is rape. But Allison would have to come to that insight on her own.

"I like to know what's going to happen next," Allison said. "Is that so bad?"

Lucille avoided the question. "And when you stick close to home, you pretty much know what's going to happen next, don't you?"

"Yes, pretty much."

"Tell me then, if you've got such good control over your life, why you still feel so bad, why you still have problems."

Something like fear clouded Allison's eyes. "I'm going to Wisconsin in September."

50

GLOUCESTER LIBRARY
GLOUCESTER, VIRGINIA 23061

"And you're afraid what might happen to you there, away from home? Afraid you might 'fall in love'?"

"Maybe. Maybe that's it."

"In such a strange new place, how will you ever be able to stay in control?"

"I see what you're saying." The disarming smile turned on. "I must be a pretty uptight person, having to control everything. Can anybody change that?"

"You might start by asking yourself what's the worst thing that could happen to you if you lost control."

Allison put her hand to her mouth. The seal-your-lips gesture was more than symbolic, for Allison made no reply. At last she said, "I feel awfully tired."

"How's your mother coming with the New York gallery? Has she signed a contract yet?"

"Yes, last Friday." Allison enthusiastically gave Lucille the details of the contract and described the current discussions concerning the timing of Annemarie's first New York show. Her mother's achievement seemed not to be one of Allison's problems.

Two calls came in on Thursday. One came from a Maywood mail carrier who reported seeing the bike and a rider answering Billy's description on Route 502 about half a mile west of Conyac. The second caller, a man who refused to identify himself, reported the body of a young man lying in a culvert beside Route 54, north of its intersection with 502. Dave sent two troopers to investigate. They examined both sides of Route 54 from the intersection with 502 north to the Massachusetts border and found nothing.

Luckily for Dave's operating budget, Friday was clear and sunny, with a fresh wind blowing from the northwest. Dave met the helicopter crew at eight in the morning at a small, semipublic airfield south of the barracks. He marked out on a large map the quadrant where they should search, then returned to the barracks and answered some calls from reporters. Without real conviction he promised them a news break in time for the evening news. TV station WXBA had got a tip about the helicopter search and they were following the search with their mobile unit. The evening news program producer asked Dave to appear at the station's studios for a live interview by WXBA's news anchorman at six that evening, whether or not the helicopter search was successful.

Dave asked Phil to call Sally, Mrs. Durk, and the Yamaha dealer to tell them about the helicopter search. Harry drove him in the barracks Jeep east along Highfields Road to its intersection with Route 502. The TV mobile unit and Maywood's four police cars were already there. Out of the windows of two of the cars the blue-gray of rifle barrels glistened in the sunlight. From the firepower displayed, the Maywood police seemed to anticipate confrontation with an armed and desperate criminal, not an eighteen-year-old local boy who might well be dead.

Dave made radio contact with the helicopter copilot. "Nothing yet," said the copilot.

In the course of the morning three times the helicopter crew thought they'd spotted the Yamaha's chrome. Once the gleam in a roadside ditch turned out to be a hubcap. In two separate sections of scrub woods fifty to a hundred feet off the highway, the gleam came from aluminum beer cans.

They broke for lunch. "When we go up again, we'll make a pass over the same territory," the pilot told Dave. "Different things show up in the afternoon sun."

It was three-thirty, a half hour before the helicopter crew was due to call it a day, when the two-way radio crackled and the copilot said: "We've got it. It's in the woods behind the Conyac farm. At the end of a trail—an old logging road, looks like."

Harry made a screeching U-turn, barely beating out the Maywood cars and the TV van. The narrow logging road was clogged with a foot-thick blanket of sodden leaves alternating with upthrust boulders and axle-breaking rain-filled potholes. Dave looked back at the Maywood police cars bouncing in single file behind him. They had no jurisdiction there. The woods were part of the Conyac farm—state property. Before stepping out of the Jeep, Dave asked Harry to try to get Rolphe on the mobile phone.

The Yamaha was half hidden by fallen leaves, and the black leather saddle was dotted with greenish-white mildew. But the bike was otherwise undamaged. It lay against the base of a swamp maple.

"That's it," said Bannerman. He turned and commanded, "Men, fan out!"

"Hold on!" Dave said. "I welcome your help, but this isn't Maywood, it's state property. I want someone here from Conyac before we go tromping over their turf."

"Hold your places," Bannerman commanded his troops.

A TV reporter and cameraman rushed forward. The cameraman photographed the Yamaha with Chief Bannerman standing beside it. "How did you know to look here?" the reporter asked.

"We received a confidential tip," Bannerman said. "I can't reveal the source."

Dave overheard the interchange and shook his head. Bannerman's unblushing appropriation of credit for the discovery was no surprise. Dave and Harry waited in the Jeep for authorization to search the woods surrounding the Conyac farm. By radio, Dave thanked the helicopter crew. The helicopter dipped in acknowledgment, then rose and headed south.

After about a ten-minute wait Rolphe came on the phone and asked Dave to hold the search until Rolphe could join them as Conyac's official representative. Dave agreed, and told Chief Bannerman and the TV reporter the reason for the delay.

Another ten minutes passed before Rolphe in his VW Rabbit pulled in beside the TV van and walked up to the Jeep. "What makes you think Billy Durk is around here?" he asked Dave.

"We're pretty sure he didn't leave the county. He didn't pick up a paycheck and we don't think he would have abandoned the new bike and run off."

"Why would he have come up this old road?"

"We don't know that he did. Somebody else might have driven the bike in here to hide it." Dave got out of the Jeep. He noted that Rolphe was wearing hiking boots. They looked incongruous with his business suit. "We'll know more if we find Billy. Can we start?"

Rolphe looked worried. "I couldn't find the form. Can I have your oral promise that you'll reimburse Conyac for any damage to Conyac property as a consequence of your activities?"

"I promise," Dave said. He turned to Bannerman. "Okay. You can deploy your men."

Bannerman directed the Maywood policemen to spread out in parties of two. Harry, carrying a camera, elected to join the two policemen searching the woods directly beyond the Yamaha. Dave, Rolphe, and Bannerman remained on the road.

In less than a minute a shout came from Harry's party and the three men ran forward. In the woods barely ten feet from the Yamaha lay the body of Billy Durk covered by a mound of fallen leaves. Dave removed just enough of the leaves to determine that animals hadn't gotten to the corpse. Because of the rain, which had obliterated all ground signs, it was impossible to tell if Billy had died there or been dragged to the spot. He lay, staring up at the tree branches overhead and the pale blue triangles of sky between the young leaves. There was no indication that a struggle had taken place or that he had felt any agony before he died. Harry and the TV cameraman photographed the body, the bike, and the surrounding area.

Dave phoned Dr. Richter, the part-time medical examiner for the state in Maywood County. Dr. Richter said he'd be there in fifteen minutes.

Bannerman ordered two Maywood cars to depart. Rolphe's VW and the TV van had to back out to the highway before the police cars could leave.

Dr. Richter arrived in an ambulance. He brushed away the rest of the leaves and the insects crawling over the viscid suntanned skin. "Looks like death was instantaneous," he said. "I'd say he's been here the better part of a week." Gently, he turned the body over. A black hole about an inch wide was visible at the base of the skull. "There's the shot that did it. He didn't know what hit him. No powder burns I can see. Fired from maybe thirty feet away. I don't see an exit hole, so the bullet could be in there." Richter stepped back while the TV cameraman, Harry, and one of the policemen took close-ups of the bullet hole. Then he motioned to the ambulance crew. They carried Billy's body back to the ambulance.

"Can you get us a report by tomorrow?" Dave asked.

"I *was* going fishing," Richter said. "I'll try." The ambulance backed out of the logging road. The diminishing wail of its siren could be heard from the highway.

Bannerman ordered his men to search the area around

the body for a gun, bullets and casings, and bullet holes. "We won't find a damn thing after all this rain," he grumbled.

Rolphe scratched his chin. "I wonder if Billy was planning to see his brother. There's no more than forty, fifty feet of woods between here and the cornfield."

Dave remembered Billy's threat to kill Colin. What if Colin had turned the tables on him? "Where would Colin get his hands on a high-powered gun?" he asked Rolphe. Colin's father had collected guns, but the gun collection had been impounded by the State's Attorney's office before the murder trial. Was it still there or had it been returned to Mae Durk?

"Where the boys get most things—if they've got the money." Rolphe turned toward his car. "You'll want to see Colin, I suppose."

"I'll be over as soon as I'm through here."

Dave turned his attention to the Yamaha. "Let's see if we can get this into the Jeep without smudging any fingerprints," he said to Harry.

"Fingerprints? After the rain and the leaves?" Harry said.

"It's a possibility."

Gripping the bike under the frame, they hoisted it into the Jeep. "If we can get these police cars out of here, you can drop me off at Conyac. Then I want you to drive over to the Durks and tell Billy's mother before she sees it on TV. Next, go to McLeods' Windrush Farm and tell Sally. Finally, go to the police lab in Morgantown and give them the bike. Then come back and pick me up." Dave was about to climb in the Jeep when he suddenly remembered. "Goddamn!" He walked over to Bannerman's car. "Could you do me a big favor?" he asked the Maywood chief. "I'm supposed to be at the WXBA studio at six for the evening news. Would you sub for me?"

"Glad to," Bannerman said. "Any stuff you want me to leave out?"

"Location of the wound. Also leave it in the air whether we found the murder weapon."

"Gotcha." Bannerman ordered the two remaining patrol cars to back out. Harry followed them out onto the highway and drove Dave to Conyac's main building.

Rolphe was waiting for him in the entrance hall. "Colin's in Dr. Dennis's office. He's pretty shook up. Dennis asked to sit in when you question Colin."

"Maybe you'd like to call in a lawyer, too," Dave said. He was too tired to be polite.

"We like to protect our boys as much as we can," Rolphe answered mildly. "But it's sort of short notice for a lawyer. Dennis said he'd tape the interview and give you a copy, if that's all right."

"It'll have to be."

Dave turned down the corridor to the psychologist's office.

Colin was sitting in the middle of the couch, hunched over, his thin shoulders trembling. His narrow face was ash-white and blotched from crying. In his faded jeans and skimpy T-shirt he looked more like twelve years old than fifteen. None of his brother's good looks had come his way, and he had his mother's diffident, apologetic manner.

Simon Dennis indicated the tape recorder on his desk. "Rolphe fill you in?"

"It's all right with me," Dave said.

"Let's give the poor kid a few minutes to settle down."

"The hell with that. Start the machine. I'll read Colin his rights while he finishes bawling." Colin lifted his head.

Dave saw the boy's eyes were dry. Dennis might be impressed by the act, but he wasn't. As soon as he heard the machine start, he did the rights bit, then began the interrogation.

"Friday, a week ago, where were you?"

"Out at the farm." Colin's voice was thin, hesitant.

"All day long?"

"Yes, sir."

"That's from when to when? What hours?"

"We start at eight and end at four."

"What do you do for lunch?"

"Bring it—in a bag."

"You work pretty hard, do you?"

"Yes, sir. Most of us."

"Not all of you. Some of the boys goof off, right?" The boy was quieting down now that Dave's questions were nonthreatening.

"Some of the guys don't like farm work, but I don't mind. It's a lot better than being cooped up in here."

"You remember talking to me on the phone—when was it? Last Monday?"

"Yes, sir."

"You said you hadn't seen your brother since a week ago Sunday. You expected to see him when he got his new motorcycle, you said, but he never showed. Right?"

"That's the last time I saw him. He was—so kind of—" The thin shoulders twitched.

"Happy?"

"Yes, sir."

"Did you ever hear that Billy was worried about your getting out of Conyac?"

The boy's eyes widened. "Worried? Why?"

It was a good act—if it was an act. "Maybe he was worried you might tell the truth about how your dad died."

Colin said nothing. His mouth hung open, sucking air.

"You're absolutely certain you didn't see your brother since the Sunday before he disappeared?" Dave's voice sharpened. Dennis gave him a warning look.

"I didn't see him. No, sir."

"Not even from that high point on the farm—where you can see over to Route 502?"

"No, sir."

"He didn't come roaring up that old logging road to see you last Friday afternoon?"

"I was working down the south end, on the disc harrow."

"But you would have heard the bike, wouldn't you, and gone over to look at it. I can ask the other boys."

"I didn't see Billy. I didn't hear him neither."

"I'll find out if you're telling me the truth," Dave said. His tone was brutally cold.

Colin's eyes shifted between Dave and Dr. Dennis. "I didn't see him," he repeated.

"That's about enough, I think," Dennis said.

Dave shrugged. "Okay, you didn't see him. Do you know of anybody who'd want to kill Billy?"

Colin shook his head and swallowed.

"Not anybody? Nobody with a grudge against him?"

"No, sir."

"Did you hear a gunshot Friday afternoon—from the woods?"

"No, sir. I told you. I was down at the other end of the farm."

"You were there all day?"

"Yes, sir."

"If Billy came out of the woods at the end of the logging road, could he see you from there?"

"I don't know. I don't think so. There's kind of a hill in between."

"You stayed in the lower field all day? You didn't leave it even once?"

"No, sir."

"I'll be talking to the other boys—" He let it hang there. "Tell me, did Billy carry a gun?"

"I don't know. Sometimes."

There was no mistaking Colin's fear. Was it only because he knew Billy had a gun or was there another reason? "What kind of gun?"

"An old Army pistol. He found it in the glove compartment in Mom's car. Dad put it there, I guess."

"But as far as you know, he didn't carry a gun on his person?"

"No, sir. He never did."

"You have any idea where Billy got a thousand dollars? That's what he put down on the bike."

"A thousand dollars?" Again the mouth hung open. "It was going to cost more than that, wasn't it?"

"What did Billy tell you it was going to cost?"

"Five thousand, he said."

"And how was Billy going to get his hands on five thousand, do you know?"

"He was getting a good job when he graduated." Colin again looked toward Dennis for support. "I don't know doing what, though."

"Did your mother visit you last Sunday?"

Colin nodded.

"Did you talk about your brother?"

"No, sir."

"Not a word? He was missing and you didn't say one word about where he might be?"

"We don't talk about Billy." Colin fixed his gaze on the floor.

Dennis rose from his desk chair. "I don't know about you, but I'm hungry. We don't get there in five minutes, we miss chow."

Colin straightened. "Can I go?"

"That'll do for now," Dave said. "But if you want to tell me more about last Friday, you let me know. And I'll be asking around, don't forget that."

Dennis put his arm over the boy's shoulders as they went to the door. "Look, Colin," he said, "if you feel bad this evening, come on over to the rec hall. Lift a couple of weights or watch the movie. I think they're showing *Butch Cassidy* tonight. And I'll be around if you need me." When Colin had disappeared up the corridor, Dennis leaned on the doorjamb. "It doesn't look like Colin's your boy," he said.

Dave didn't care much for Dr. Dennis, mainly because he suspected Dennis had encouraged Lucille to get the divorce. "Too soon to say that," he said. "If there's one thing I know Colin's good at, it's lying. He lied going in and he lied going out about his dad's murder and no one could shake him, not the judge, not even Lucille."

"Yes. Well—"

"I'd like to talk with the farm manager. Where do I find him?"

"He lives on the farm—the old farmhouse goes with the job. It's at the south end of Skunk Hollow Road."

"I'll see if I can catch him." They had reached the main entrance. "Do you live here now?" he asked Dennis.

"No. The staff takes turns on weekends. It just happens to be my turn."

"Do the farm boys work on Saturdays?"

"Not usually."

"I may send some troopers over to interrogate them. Otherwise I imagine you'll be hearing from the Major Crime Unit investigators."

"Whatever you say." Dennis turned back up the corridor.

Harry was waiting in the Jeep.

"How'd Mae Durk take it?" Dave asked.

"Tough. And the girl was worse."

"Find out anything at the lab?" Dave climbed into the Jeep.

"Not until tomorrow. They might get something off the handlebars because the leaves were covering them." Harry turned right onto 502. "What did Colin say?"

"That kid's the three monkeys—hears nothing, sees nothing, says nothing."

Harry laughed. "You believe him?"

"Not even a little bit." Dave sighed. "We've got one more stop. Turn left up ahead. The farm manager. His house is on Skunk Hollow."

"I better call my wife."

"You can call from the farmhouse."

The farm manager was waiting for them on the porch. He put his hand out. "I'm Lube Starr. You're—?"

"Lieutenant Littlejohn and Trooper Walsh."

"C'mon inside. Kinda buggy out here." Lube Starr led them into a living room furnished with a bright new tan tweed living-room suite. "Have a seat."

Dave and Harry sat on the couch. Lube sat on the edge of the overstuffed chair, as if he might be uneasy about soiling it. He was a scrawny, black-haired man, about forty, and spoke with a Maine twang. "What you want to know?" he asked.

"Everything you can remember about last Friday afternoon. Colin Durk's brother was murdered in the woods about forty feet off the north end of the farm."

"I heard."

"Were any of the boys working there last Friday?"

"No. That's high there, so we got that planted a week ago. In corn. You don't have to worry there about wash-out."

"Did you see any of the boys in the cornfield, walking around there?"

"No—but that don't mean they didn't. I can't keep an eye on every one of them."

"Are there security people watching the boys?"

"No. It's the honor system. I been here eight years. A few take off. Not many."

"Did you notice where Colin was during the after-noon?"

"He was working the disc harrow in the south field. That's maybe a thousand feet from the cornfield. I would have noticed if he was gone off the harrow the time it'd take to walk up there and back."

"Were you out with the boys the entire afternoon?"

"Well, no. I couldn't say that."

Harry asked if he could use the phone. Lube directed him to the phone table at the foot of the stairs and Harry called his wife.

"When the boys stop for lunch, where do they usually go?" Dave continued.

"Sometimes they go over to the brook, try a little fish-ing. Piece of string, a hook, a bit of bologna from their sandwiches. Every once in a while they catch something. Nothing worth eating. Some of the boys go across the road. There's a ball field there, and they play ball. They're only kids, you know."

"Do any of the boys go into the woods at lunch?"

"A couple. Dopers. I can smell it when the wind blows right. But as long as they work good, I don't rat on them."

"Has it ever happened that some of the boys stayed in the woods all afternoon? Didn't come back to work after lunch?"

"You always get some no-goods. I get wise to them, they get no more farm days."

"How many days does a boy work on the farm?"

"Two. The rest of the time they got school. The boy you're asking about worked Tuesday, Friday."

"So there's a steady turnover of boys working on the farm."

"You might say that."

Dave noticed Harry looking worried. "Thanks for your help. If you particularly remember any boys going in or near the woods last Friday, please call me at the barracks."

Lube Starr stood on the porch as Dave and Harry got in the Jeep. "Colin's a good worker," he said. "I'd hate to lose him."

At the barracks Harry got into his own car and sped away. Dave, who had no wife to hurry home to, went into his office and found three reporters waiting for him. The day wasn't over yet.

CHAPTER
4

One of the country's best Italian restaurants is in Danbury, Connecticut. Saturday evening, over fettucine and scampi, Dave told Lucille all he could reveal about Billy's death. "Harry spent the day at Conyac questioning the farm boys. They knocked some holes in Colin's story."

"Just because he lied about his father's murder doesn't mean he's lying about this," Lucille said.

"He said he never left the south end, and two boys said he went up to the woods beyond the cornfield around the middle of the afternoon. That sounds like lying to me."

"Did the boys say they saw his brother and the motorcycle?"

"No. There's a rise and you can't see the edge of the woods from the south field."

She frowned. "Why so hostile toward Colin?"

"I'm not hostile, just looking for the truth." Dave leaned forward, a strand of fettucine dangling from his fork. "And this time I'm going to find it. You know why?"

"Why?"

"Because every time somebody gets away with murder—and that's what the Durk brothers more or less did—it encourages other people to sneer at the law, to see if they can't get away with murder, too. It's an invitation to anarchy."

"And we can't have anarchy, can we?" Whenever Dave waxed philosophical, she responded with levity, a reaction she regretted because it hinted at patronization. But she couldn't help herself. "So meek little Colin has set off a murder binge in Maywood County."

"I didn't say that." When Dave was irritated, his skin paled rather than reddened. In the candlelight of the restaurant table his broad cheeks were the pale yellow of parchment. "All I'm saying is that Colin isn't going to get away with lying this time."

"Are you going to arrest him?"

"He's not going anyplace from where he's at."

"How do you think it happened?"

"Here's how I see it. Around three, three-thirty in the afternoon, Colin caught sight of Billy on the new bike riding along 502. You can see the highway from the cornfield. So he went into the woods and along the old logging road until he and Billy met up. The brothers had an argument. Billy brought out a gun and Colin took it away from him and killed him."

"The newspapers said there was no sign of a struggle."

"Hard to tell after all the rain."

"So then Colin left his brother dead in the woods and calmly walked back to the field where he was working. What did he do with the gun? He couldn't keep it on his person, could he? He must have thrown it into the woods somewhere."

"We'll find it." Dave speared a shrimp and put it whole into his mouth.

"I don't think you will," Lucille said mildly.

"Christ, you're a know-it-all bitch."

"That's news?"

They laughed, and Lucille asked him how his Russian was coming—a less explosive subject.

Search for the murder weapon continued through the weekend. Troopers, Maywood police, local constables, and detectives from the state's Major Crime Unit all took part in the search. The brook that ran through the farm was combed from end to end. Not an inch of the upper and lower fields escaped attention. The cottage where Colin lived with seven other boys had no corner left undisturbed. Items of contraband were found, but not a gun. The harrow and other farm machinery as well as the shed where they were stored got a thorough going-over.

Although no weapon had been found, Dave went to Conyac on Monday morning to interrogate Colin further. Rolphe had arranged for Conyac's lawyer, Mr. Rubin, a small round man with eager brown eyes, to be there to guard Colin's rights.

"About what time was it Friday afternoon that you saw Billy riding along 502?" Dave asked abruptly.

"I didn't see Billy Friday," Colin said. His manner was stoic, as if he expected accusation and mistreatment, even physical abuse, but he'd hold to his story nonetheless.

"Two boys saw you go up to the cornfield Friday afternoon."

"I never left the south field." Colin's eyes focused on an oil painting of a red barn on the wall opposite. He looked neither at Dave nor at Mr. Rubin.

"We know that you saw your brother Friday afternoon," Dave continued with no change of expression. "That's some bike, isn't it?"

Colin's eyes met Dave's and brightened for a fraction of a second before he returned to stolid contemplation of the painting. "I didn't see the bike," he said.

"You must have seen the bike. You saw Billy riding it along 502 and then you saw him with it on the road into the woods. We have witnesses."

"I didn't see the bike," Colin repeated. "I didn't see Billy."

Dave caught a warning glance from the lawyer. He bent toward the boy. "You know, you're not protecting Billy this time. He's dead." He made his voice warmer, more sympathetic. "We've got enough to put you in jail now. Or, with just one word, we could see you're off the farm. That's if you keep on lying. We know you saw Billy." Dave paused and looked worried. "Maybe you got in an argument. Was that what happened?"

"I didn't see him."

"Maybe you saw somebody shoot him. If you did, why would you want to protect someone who killed your brother, someone who wasn't a member of your family? Why would you want to protect him?"

Colin's eyes remained fixed on the painting. "I stayed in the south field. I didn't see anybody."

Although Dave knew now that the boy was lying, somehow he felt sorry for him. Maybe it was Colin's stoic assumption that no matter what he said or did, he would suffer. Colin would continue to lie because he had no expectation that the truth would lead to justice. "I'd hate to have you taken off the farm," Dave said. "I know how much you like it."

Colin's shoulders sagged. He said nothing.

"I tell you what. You promise not to run away and you can still work on the farm Tuesdays and Fridays. Anyway, it'd be dumb to run away. We'd find you and you'd be booked for Billy's murder in ten seconds." He tried to catch Colin's gaze, without success. "How about it? Promise you won't try to make a break?"

Colin nodded.

"Then, as soon as you decide to tell the truth, you let Mr. Rubin here know and he'll tell me. Okay?"

"I'm telling the truth," Colin said, his eyes still on the painting.

Dave decided he could go no further. Lacking the murder weapon, his threat to put Colin in jail was a bluff. He turned to the lawyer and shrugged.

On Monday afternoon the preliminary autopsy report came in. Death had been instantaneous. A .44 Magnum bullet had pierced the brain in an upward arc through the left prefrontal lobe and lodged in the skull. The absence of powder burns and the size of the bullet hole meant the gun had been fired from a distance of approximately thirty feet. The murderer might have been shorter than Billy, or had crouched when firing, or had stood on lower ground, or Billy had been bending down when he was shot.

Dave called the state's attorney's office. He spoke with Sandra Murphy, the ambitious young assistant S.A. who had worked on the Durk case.

"Was there a Magnum in the Durk gun collection?" he asked.

"Just a second. I'll have to look in the files." Dave waited several minutes before Sandra returned to the phone. "Yes, a .357 Magnum, but—"

"But what?"

"We returned the guns to Mrs. Durk last month—all except the Magnum. Somebody liberated the Magnum while the collection was in the safe. It happens."

"Any idea who the liberator was?"

"Probably a cop. You know how nutty cops are about guns."

"I'm a cop," Dave reminded her. "Thanks anyway."

Had Billy got his hands on the missing gun? Dave continued to favor the scenario he'd outlined to Lucille, but the first step in proving it was to put the gun in Billy's possession.

He asked Phil to get a court order allowing the bank to trace Billy's thousand-dollar check. He also wanted to look at Billy's bank account.

Tuesday morning he went with Harry to see Mae Durk.

Harry rapped on the kitchen door. "C'mon in," said a man's voice.

Marty Grunewald, the widow's brother, was sitting beside her at the large square kitchen table. The table was covered with a torn and spotted red plastic tablecloth. "Mae asked me to come over," he explained. He motioned Dave and Harry to sit at the table. The high-backed wood chairs were painted puce-green enamel. Where the paint had chipped away, previous coatings of red and cream-colored enamel showed through.

The green paint felt gummy. "We're sorry to bother you," Dave said. Mae Durk sat at the table, placid, her hands folded in front of a coffee cup. How did you interrogate a woman whose husband and son had both met death by violence within the year?

"Would you like some coffee?" she asked. "It's fresh made."

"Thanks." He looked to Harry, who nodded. "We'd appreciate it."

She rose and moved slowly, almost dreamily. She took a chipped blue enamel coffeepot from the stove and two brown mugs from a dish drain beside the old-fashioned sink. As she poured the coffee, she looked at the troopers mildly, without a hint of curiosity.

The coffee was strong and bitter. "Remember when I called you last week—when Billy was missing?" Dave began. "You said you were sure he was all right. Any reason why you were sure?"

"He's a good boy." She seemed unaware that she'd used the present tense.

Her brother looked worried. "He's dead," he said bluntly. "You can't expect Mae to say anything bad about him."

Dave turned his attention to the prosperous farmer sitting beside him. Marty's blue work clothes were freshly ironed and spotless. He bore no detectable resemblance to his frail sister in her soiled housedress and frayed cardigan. "Would you," Dave asked him, "say that Billy might have been involved in something that was dangerous or illegal?"

Marty avoided his sister's bland stare. "Yes, he could have been. He thought he was pretty smart, had it all figured out. He didn't give a damn for anybody, including his mother."

"Oh, Marty," Mae said, "he's young."

Harry brought the coffee mug to his lips and swallowed as if he were having trouble getting the liquid down.

"You know, Mrs. Durk," Dave said, "Billy deposited a check for a thousand dollars a week ago Friday, the last day anybody saw him. Was there an envelope in your mail that day, addressed to Billy?"

"A week ago Friday?" She rubbed the bridge of her nose. "That's right! He came home from school early and stood out in front waiting for the mail. Then, when he got it, he went right away."

"You didn't see what he got in the mail?"

"He didn't come in the house. He left the other mail in the box—ads and that sort of thing."

"How'd he get home from school?"

"He had the car. He didn't like to take the bus. But he left the car here after he picked up his mail."

"Did he ever mention to you that he was expecting a large amount of money?"

"No." She thought a moment, then repeated: "No."

"He wouldn't," Marty said. "Whatever he made he kept for himself. That's why I wouldn't let him work for me. All for Number One, nothing for anybody else. And look what it got him."

"Marty, please." Mae Durk passed reddened fingers over her eyes. "The police doctor said we can't have the funeral until Friday."

"What about phone calls?" Dave continued, his voice rough because he hated having to question her. "From the time Billy returned from Florida to when he disappeared, were there any phone calls from strangers, any long-distance calls?"

"He got a call from California, but it wasn't a stranger. It was Mr. Craig. He lives here in Highfields. I've met him."

"Did you notice how Billy acted when he talked on the phone with Mr. Craig? Did he act happy? Angry? Upset?"

"Oh, he was happy. Mr. Craig took an interest in Billy. He was going to give him a job when he graduated, a good job."

"In the movies? Doing what?"

"I don't know. Billy said it was going to pay good."

"Did Billy ever talk about becoming an actor?"

"Yes, he did. But he wasn't going to acting school. Mr. Craig said he should stay natural. What he needed to know Mr. Craig would teach him."

"About when did Billy start to talk about working in the movies?"

"After—after the trial. That's how Mr. Craig and Billy got acquainted. Mr. Craig saw his picture in the papers and he called here and said he was a neighbor." Suddenly she crumpled. "He was so happy after the call."

Dave nodded at Harry and they both rose. "Just one more question, Mrs. Durk," Dave said. "You got your husband's gun collection back from the state. Is it here in the house?"

"I sold it. I won't have no guns around. Not anymore." Her lips quivered.

"Isn't there an old Army pistol in your car?"

"It's all rusted. It's not worth anything."

"Would you mind if we took a look at it when we leave?"

"That's all right."

Dave looked uncomfortably toward the stairs. "We have to search Billy's room."

She nodded. "It's the first room."

Harry followed him up the stairs.

It was a teenage boy's room. Posters of rock stars on the walls and closet door. The bed unmade. Sneakers, dirty socks, and schoolbooks on the floor. A faded rag rug crumpled up in a corner. In another corner a three-drawer oak desk, piled high with *Penthouse* magazines. Harry searched under the magazine pile and in the desk drawers. Dave searched the bureau drawers and the closet. At the back of the closet shelf he found a brass water pipe. It looked unused. In the pocket of a down jacket was a sheet of folded notepaper with a single telephone number written in pencil—897-4042. Searching under the bed, under the mattress, in the hot-air register, and in the overhead light fixture yielded nothing.

Downstairs, Dave showed the notepaper to Mrs. Durk. "Is that Billy's writing?"

"Yes."

"Do you recognize the number?"

She shook her head. "It must be around here, though." The Highfields exchange was 897.

Marty stood at the back door. The telephone number meant nothing to him either. "Got to get back to work," he said to his sister. "You come on over to eat tonight, okay? Annemarie says you shouldn't be here by yourself."

Dave heard the tractor start up in the dirt yard behind the house. "Thank you, Mrs. Durk," he said. "We're going to find who shot your son; don't you worry."

Her eyes were vacant of understanding. "Don't tell Colin," she said.

"Don't tell him what?" Harry said as he held the door open.

"About Billy. Don't tell him." She crossed her arms on the table and stared past the two troopers, into distant blankness.

"Please call the barracks if you need anything," Dave said. "Please."

A ten-year-old Dodge two-door was parked in the gravel driveway at the side of the house. Harry opened the right front door and looked in the glove compartment. The gun was at the bottom, covered by rags and maps. With a handkerchief to shield the gun from his prints, he withdrew the World War II pistol and showed it to Dave.

"Doesn't look like much," Dave said, "but we better get it over to Morgantown."

"I'll take it over first thing tomorrow," Harry said.

At the barracks Dave asked Phil to trace the telephone number and Phil handed him a list of calls: two reporters,

Rolphe from Conyac, Chief Bannerman, and the Morgantown lab. He called Morgantown first.

"Are Colin Durk's fingerprints on the bike?"

"No. Only Billy's."

"Damn!"

Rolphe told him that four detectives from the Major Crime Unit office had been at Conyac that morning and had interrogated every single boy there. If they had discovered anything, they hadn't told Rolphe.

Chief Bannerman said he was continuing to search for the murder weapon. Was there anything else Dave would like him to do?

"Your men know all the merchants up and down 502," Dave said. "What we need is a canvass of all the stores and houses starting with the motorcycle dealer on 54, then over to McLeod's Highfields real-estate office, then east on 502 until the intersection with the logging road into the Conyac farm. Both sides of 502. See if you can find anybody who saw Billy that Friday afternoon, on or off the bike."

"Gotcha," said Bannerman.

Dave crossed off the reporters' names. On the rare occasions when a major crime was committed in Troop B territory, Dave preferred to let the State Police information officer handle the media.

He phoned Sam Burns, one of Highfields's three constables. "Sam, we've learned that Billy left his home on foot around two Friday afternoon. He was on his way over to the bank. Can you check around and see if anybody gave him a lift?"

"Glad to," Sam said.

Phil buzzed him. "The phone number belongs to Ellis Somers."

"You know anything about him?"

"I better come in," Phil said.

Phil bent stiffly over Dave's desk. The thin strands of graying brown hair covering his bald spot fell forward over his eyes. "You never heard of Ellis Somers?" he asked in a half-whisper.

"Why?"

"I thought you were interested in the theater. He's a famous set designer."

"What's wrong with that? Why the hush-hush?"

"He's gay. He lives with a young guy, blond, big muscles. The blond does all the work around the house, gardens, cooks, too. I can't remember his name."

"Where's the house?"

"It's across the road from the Durks. A nice old colonial, at least from the outside."

"Are Somers and his friend weekenders?"

"They used to be, but now I heard they live in Highfields year-round. Somers is retired, I hear."

"He's an older man then. About how old?"

"In his sixties at least, but he looks younger."

"Is he a friend of Garrison Craig?"

Phil twisted his mouth. "They're about the same age and they know each other, but I don't think they're friends. The gays stick together and Craig is definitely not gay."

Dave was annoyed by Phil's raised eyebrow. Unstopped, Phil could run on for hours. "Thanks, Phil. That's a help."

Why would Billy Durk have the telephone number of a gay set designer who happened to be a neighbor? He added Ellis Somers's name to his list of names for interrogation. Garrison Craig, the Farnols in New York—and he would have to go a second round with Sally McLeod. It couldn't be avoided. If his initial scenario was wrong, he had to find out who would want to kill Billy and why. His most obvious lead to an answer was the thousand-dollar check. As soon as he knew the source of the check, he'd be in better shape to tackle his list. In the meantime, Bannerman's men or the MCU detectives might come up with something that pointed to Colin and his troubles would be over.

Dave phoned Sandra Murphy. "Would you mind telling me why MCU sent four men over to Conyac this morning?" he said. "I'm not guarding my turf, but I'd appreciate being kept informed."

"Oh, sorry. They were supposed to call you."

"Frankly, I couldn't mount the manpower to do that kind of interrogation, but I don't remember asking for your help."

"We were answering a citizen complaint," Sandra said.

"A what?"

"A citizen complaint. One of Conyac's neighbors, a Mrs. Garson. She lives in a house across from the south end of the farm. She saw your murder suspect working at the farm this morning and she was outraged. What was going to stop Colin from jumping the fence and killing her? So we sent the detectives over to calm her nerves." She laughed lightly. "I figured you were going to request it sooner or later, so why wait? Incidentally, whatever possessed you to let Colin keep working on the farm?"

"The farm manager didn't want to lose him. He's a good worker and he isn't about to run. That's not his style. He stands in one place, keeps his mouth shut, and takes it, whatever it is we're dishing out. You ought to know that."

She laughed again. "Do I ever."

"The MCU turn up anything?"

"A couple of boys thought they knew where the gun was hidden. They were just brown-nosing."

"That gun is there somewhere. I'll lay even money it's the one liberated from your office."

"No on both counts. Bannerman has gone over every inch of woods and fields and every other place he can think of. We can't indict without a weapon, unless we get something else. As for the missing Magnum, nobody saw Billy Durk anywhere near this office since his brother's trial."

"If someone gave him the gun by mistake, they wouldn't admit it."

"Probably not. But somebody would have noticed if Billy was in the building. There are a lot of people here, in and out."

"Even at lunchtime?"

"Yes, even at lunchtime."

"Try to keep me informed, will you? I'd hate to see us tripping over each other. It wouldn't look good."

"You're so right."

CHAPTER

5

"I don't know what to do about Sally," Allison said, midway through their Wednesday session.

"Hadn't you stopped being friends because of Billy?"

"Now that Billy's gone, she needs a shoulder to cry on." Allison's tone was cold.

"Did you go to Sally's house or did she come to see you?" It was important to know if Allison had broken her self-imposed after-school isolation.

"I see her at school. She can't stop crying. It's embarrassing."

"Is that all you feel about her grief?"

Allison looked at her coolly. "Whatever I say here is confidential, isn't it?"

"Of course."

"It isn't just grief. Sally feels guilty. She says she's sure she caused Billy's death and she can't sleep or eat. She looks sick."

"Would you like me to speak to her grandparents?"

"She made me promise not to tell anybody. I tried to make some sense with her, to find out how she thinks she caused Billy's murder, but all she says is, 'I know you know, Allison, but you mustn't tell anybody.' The truth is, Dr. Esker, I don't know how she could possibly be guilty, so I couldn't tell anybody even if I wanted to."

Was Allison's wide-eyed candor a shade overdone? Might not Allison be projecting onto Sally her own guilty thoughts regarding Billy? Allison must have often, in the three years since he had raped her, wished him dead.

"You said last week, before Billy was found, that you were sure he'd been killed. Now that you know he's been murdered, how do you feel?"

"Satisfied."

"You don't feel even a little bit sorry that someone so young met death by violence?"

"He deserved to die."

Allison's composure was chilling. Lucille wondered if it was ever going to be possible to penetrate it. "Sally doesn't think he deserved to die, does she?"

"I told you. He made her his slave."

"Do you know other people who think as you do—that he deserved to be killed?"

"A few."

"Such as?"

Allison glanced toward the door. "I can't name names."

"But you do know of such people."

"Yes."

"Including his brother—Colin?"

Allison smiled. "That's ridiculous. Colin worshiped Billy. He was another one of his slaves."

"So you think, no matter what Billy did, Colin would accept it."

"He went to jail for him, didn't he?"

The shallowness of Allison's emotional reaction to Billy's death was consistent with her general state of depression. Lucille would have liked to probe at least the edges of the rape experience, but Billy's murder made that inadvisable.

"Sally has come to you for help. How do you feel about that?"

"Strange. We used to be best friends, until she fell in love with Billy. She thought Billy liked me better and I'd take him away from her. It didn't do a bit of good for me to tell her that I couldn't stand him. She was so jealous it was funny. I mean, how could you take her seriously?"

"And you weren't envious of her—of her ability to fall in love? You told me you missed being able to fall in love."

The silence lasted several seconds. "Not envious. Sad," she said.

"Sad for yourself or for Sally?"

"Both. We were really close, you know. Everybody at school now is so—so phony. The teachers, the students—there's not a single honest person at Maywood High."

"Except Sally?"

"Not even Sally. Not anymore." Her voice was low and despairing.

"So it must be hard for you to help her if you think she's dishonest or insincere."

"I'm only a crying towel. That's all she wants me for."

"Do you feel you're not any good to anybody?"

"Yes."

"And nobody would miss you if you were gone?"

"Yes."

"That's your depression speaking inside you. Those feelings have no connection with reality. You probably recognize that's true, from time to time. And when your depression is gone—and I promise you it will go—those feelings will go with it." Lucille put her arm across Allison's shoulder.

They sat there on the couch in silence. At length Allison looked at her wristwatch and said, "My time is up."

Lucille nodded and followed Allison to the door of her office. "See you next week," she said with a cheer that even she recognized as phony.

Thursday was publication day for the *Maywood Weekly Leader*. The banner headline read MURDER NO. 2 FOR COLIN DURK? The head over the story in the right-hand column read SUSPECT HAD OPPORTUNITY, MOTIVE, and the subhead under that: SEARCH FOR MURDER WEAPON CONTINUES.

Dave read the story with disgust. Details that he had wanted to keep confidential, such as the make of the gun and the location of the bullet hole, were revealed. The leaks could have come from Conyac, Dr. Richter's office, or the Morgantown lab. By Friday morning all the daily newspapers and the wire services would repeat the story, and Colin would be as good as convicted of his brother's murder in the mind of the public. Colin Durk—patricide and fratricide, if you wanted to get fancy about it. Oedipus was small change compared to Highfields's Colin Durk.

For Lucille, the newspaper story represented another dilemma. It was important that Dave be told of Allison's conviction that Colin would never voluntarily harm his brother. She'd breached confidentiality to tell Dave of Billy's threat against Colin. Why couldn't confidentiality be breached to establish Colin's innocence?

Unfortunately, there was no law to support her. And if she presented Allison's conclusion as her own, Dave would disregard it as just another example of her softheadedness when it came to criminals.

Early Thursday afternoon Dave tried to reach Ellis Somers. No one answered. Garrison Craig was reported to be on his way back from the Coast, but had still not arrived in High-fields.

The New York City police had given Dave the Farnols' address and unlisted phone number. Phil tried the number. Again no answer.

Dave asked him to call Morgantown. "Any news on the Army pistol I sent over Tuesday?" he asked Doc Prentiss, chief of the ballistics lab.

"A couple of smudged prints but nothing identifiable. The gun's worthless. We had to soak it to open it up. A single bullet was stuck in there like cement."

Dave left the barracks and went to the Highfields bank. Helen Wadsworth told him that Billy's check had been issued by Columbus Educational Enterprises, Inc., of 717 Decatur Avenue, Columbus, Ohio. From the bank he phoned Phil and asked him to put in a long-distance call to Ohio's Secretary of State to get the names of the Ohio corporation's directors. The signature on the check was "Martha Davenport, Treasurer."

Helen gave Dave copies of Billy's checking-account statements for the preceding six months. He sat in a chair next to an unused desk and looked through the statements. The only sizable deposit in the entire six-month period was the thousand dollars deposited on the day Billy died. Every previous week on a Monday he'd deposited fifty dollars, apparently part of his paycheck from Rick Hallberg's trash-removal service. Billy's largest withdrawal was two hundred dollars, made the last day of March. The money could have been taken out for the spring vacation trip to Florida.

He called the McLeods to make sure Sally was home. Rose McLeod answered the phone. "Yes, Sally's here. She just got home from school."

"I have to question her about Billy," Dave said. "I've held off as long as I can."

"I'll tell her."

He found her in the sunroom. Her eyes were dry, but her face was drawn and gray. The look she gave him as he stepped into the bright, sun-filled room was despairing.

"I don't see how I can help," she said.

Dave pulled his chair closer. "Let's start with the check. I've learned that it came from a company in Ohio called Columbus Educational Enterprises. The check was signed by somebody named Martha Davenport. The names mean anything to you?"

"No. Not at all." She shook her head in bewilderment. "From Ohio? That's strange."

"You promised to tell me what Billy did to earn the money if something happened to him."

She raised her head in alarm. "No, I didn't."

"There's no reason to feel afraid, Sally. If it was something illegal—"

"No, it was all right, it was legal," she said hurriedly. "Billy told you that."

"Yes, I remember. But even if it wasn't, the law can't touch him now."

"It was educational, like the company name says."

"What kind of education? Was it an educational film? Did he act in an educational film? While you were in Florida?"

She nodded.

"What kind of educational film?" Dave persisted.

"I don't know."

"But you were there. In Florida. Are you sure you don't know?"

"I don't know," she repeated.

"Was Mr. Craig the director?"

She nodded.

"But you don't know what the film was about, what subject it covered."

She stared at him. Fear clouded her eyes.

"Let's go back to that Friday afternoon," Dave said, settling back in the chair. "Can you remember who was in the real-estate office besides yourself?"

"Tess Sandford was there. She came in from showing a property."

"Anybody else?"

"No. I take over from Flora, Mrs. Warburg, so she can be home when her kids get back from school. She was gone before—before Billy—"

"Was your grandfather there?"

"No. He almost never comes to the Highfields office. He's mostly in the Maywood office." She gave a wan smile.

"Did you leave the office with Billy?"

"No. He just came in and then went away."

"What exactly did he say?"

"He said, 'I got it!'"

"And what did you say?"

"I don't know. 'That's great!' Something like that."

"And that's all you said to each other?"

"Well, Tess was there listening. Besides, we were— we were going out Friday night." She shivered and clutched her arms.

"What were you going to do Friday night?"

"Nothing much. Ride around. Go to Pete's house— Pete Hallberg always has a bunch of kids over, listen to records. Billy works for Pete's father." Suddenly her eyes filled. "Worked."

"Would you have ridden over to Pete's on the new motorcycle?"

"Maybe. So everyone could see it. Buy maybe I would have taken my car. I'm a little scared about riding piggyback at night."

Dave nodded. Sally wasn't the daring type, but he was sure that if Billy had ordered her to sit behind him on the bike, she would have done so, no matter how dangerous the road, how dark the night. "Tell me," he continued, "when Billy left the office, did you notice if he stopped to talk to anyone before he got on his bike?"

Sally shook her head. "He just rode off down 502. That's all I saw."

"Right away?"

She frowned. "I had to answer the phone, and then when I hung up I saw him through the front window getting on his bike."

"About how long was the phone conversation?"

"About three or four minutes. It was someone who'd seen an ad for a house in North Maywood and I had to get out the card from the North Maywood file—I only keep the Highfields file on my desk—and that took a couple of minutes."

"If Billy had been talking to anyone outside the office while you were on the phone, would you have noticed?"

"I wasn't looking out the window. I was looking at the card."

Dave allowed himself a sigh. He felt sure Sally was telling the truth. At the same time, she was hiding something—something that frightened her.

"Can you think of anyone who might have had a reason to want Billy dead?"

She shook her head.

"In the Durk murder trial it came out that Mr. Durk had taught Billy and Colin how to use firearms, and they were both expert marksmen. Can you think of any of Billy's friends or classmates who were interested in guns or did target shooting?"

"Pete's the only one I can think of. He and Billy used to go over to the dump and shoot rats. They were doing the town a favor, but one of the constables made them stop."

"Do you know which constable that was?"

"No."

"Do you remember what kind of gun Billy used to shoot the rats?"

"No. I don't like guns." Again she shivered. "I wish—" she began and put her hands over her face.

"Thanks for your help, Sally," Dave said. "I'll let myself out."

As he left the sunroom he noticed Rose McLeod standing at the foot of the stairs. He planned to interrogate the McLeods eventually. Now was as good a time as any. "Excuse me, Mrs. McLeod. Could you spare a few minutes?"

"Of course. Would you like a cup of coffee or a drink?"

"No, thanks." He followed her into the long living room, furnished with American Colonial antiques.

She led him to two armchairs flanking a candlestand in front of a bay window. "Did Sally tell you anything useful?"

"Possibly. But I felt she was hiding something—something that frightened her. Do you have any idea what she could be frightened of?"

"Nothing except that the way Billy died—" Her voice was harsh and the look she gave Dave was accusatory. "That would frighten anybody."

Dave nodded. "But it was something more than that, something secret."

"I've no idea, then." Her jaw tightened.

"You and Mr. McLeod were upset when your granddaughter went to Florida with Billy without your permission. How did you feel about Billy when they returned?"

"No better, if that's what you mean. We still didn't trust him. He was a sly, deceitful boy. I grieve for his poor mother, not for him."

"Where were you last Friday afternoon?"

"Playing bridge at Peg Tomlinson's house on Willow Ridge. There used to be eight of us. Now we're just four. We've met for bridge every Friday for ages."

"Was Mr. McLeod home last Friday?"

"No. He usually goes to the office Fridays. Tuesdays and Fridays are his usual days." Her voice softened. "Are you going to question him, too?"

"Yes. Is he home?"

"He's in his study. He may be sleeping." She adjusted her bifocals and leaned toward Dave. "I hope I can trust you to keep this to yourself."

"Of course."

"Andy tries to go on the way he always did, but he can't. He has cancer. It's not a fast cancer, it's slow, but it could speed up any time. He doesn't want anybody to know about it. His pride. He has tremendous pride, you know."

"He's a fine man."

"I'll see if he's awake."

Dave followed her out of the living room. She entered a room off the center hall. After a minute or so, she reappeared. "He just woke up, but he says come in and he'll be happy to answer your questions."

Dave found Andy McLeod sitting on a tufted leather couch, a bright-colored afghan across his lap. With his fingers he was combing his thin gray hair, mussed from his nap.

"How can I help you?" Andy motioned Dave to the chair behind the leather-topped mahogany desk.

"I'll try to make it brief," Dave said. "Sally gave me the impression she was hiding something, and it was something that frightened her. Do you know what it is?"

"No mystery, no mystery at all. Billy frightened her. She was obsessed with him, and an obsession is frightening. Isn't that what a psychologist would tell you? Then there's the way he died. Naturally she's frightened."

"But you can't think of anything else?"

Andy's look sharpened. "Why? Do you think whoever killed Billy might come after Sally?"

"It's possible."

"Should I hire someone, a bodyguard? Is that what you're saying?"

"No, no." Dave tried to look reassuring. "I don't think Sally is in any real danger."

"Anything else you'd like to ask me?"

Dave took out his notepad. "I understand you were in your Maywood office last Friday afternoon. Were you there all afternoon?"

"No. At one-thirty I left the office with Mr. and Mrs. Edwin Olin—he's an IBM executive. The Olins came down from Binghamton to look at property here because Mr. Olin is being transferred to Connecticut. I showed them three places, winding up with the Davis place in Highfields Landing, a beautiful house on a nice piece of land. I have an idea the Olins are going to make an offer."

"After showing houses to the Olins, did you come home or return to the office?"

"I went back to the office."

"About what time was that?"

"Around a quarter to four. Give or take five minutes."

"Did you notice Billy on his brand-new motorcycle while you were driving east on 502?"

"I didn't notice much of anything." Andy grinned. "I was thinking about the Davis place and the Olins. I get a lot of satisfaction out of finding the right buyer for a lovely piece of property like that."

"Were you in your office the rest of the afternoon?"

"Yes. I came home at the usual hour, around five."

Dave made a note of the Olins' name, address, and business connection. "Do you own a gun, Andy?"

He nodded. "A small revolver. I keep it in a drawer beside my bed. Luckily, I've never had to use it."

Dave stood. "Thanks for your help."

"No trouble." Andy accompanied him to the front

door. "If you have any more questions, I'll be happy to answer them. And I'll keep an eye on Sally, just in case."

Back at the barracks Dave added Pete Hallberg's name to his list of people he needed to interrogate. When Harry came in from patrol, he asked Harry to find out if Tess Sandford had noticed Billy speaking to anyone outside the McLeods' Highfields office Friday afternoon. He gave Phil the task of contacting Mrs. Tomlinson and the Olins of Binghamton to confirm the McLeods' stories.

Lucille was just out the door Friday evening, on her way to meet Mavis Sprague and see a movie, when she heard her phone ring. She went back into the house and picked up the receiver. It was Allison's mother.

"Dr. Esker, can you come over to the house right away, please? It's an emergency. Please. I don't know what to do."

"I'll be right there." She hung up and rang Mavis. Luckily Mavis hadn't yet left. "I've got an emergency," Lucille said. "I hope you'll go and tell me all about it."

"Understood," Mavis said.

Annemarie was waiting for her at the door of the farmhouse. "See what she's done," she said. An aura of hysteria enveloped her.

Lucille walked past her into the living room. Allison stood in the archway leading to the dining room. Her face was made up like a clown's, a broad red grin painted over her lips. Her eyes were outlined thickly in black, and on her white-painted cheeks she had drawn black teardrops. She was giggling.

"What brings you here?" she said to Lucille. "Did you come to see my artwork?" She pointed with both hands toward her face.

Annemarie sobbed and ran from the room.

"Where's your stepfather?" Lucille asked, and took a seat on the couch.

"Downstairs, in the rumpus room, watching TV. Isn't that a hilarious name—rumpus room? That's what I've done—made a rumpus. A real honest-to-god rumpus. Isn't that hilarious?" Her giggling continued.

Lucille patted the cushion beside her on the couch. "How about sitting down and telling me about it."

Allison cocked her head. "There's nothing to tell. I just wanted to give everyone a laugh. Isn't that what everyone wants? I'm supposed to be happy, cheerful. Being depressed is terrible. Nobody should be depressed."

"C'mon. Allison. Sit down," Lucille said.

Picking her feet high off the ground, as if she were walking through slime, Allison approached the couch. Directly in front of Lucille she curtsied, then twirled in a complete circle and sat with a thump on the couch. "You are not amused," she said in an exaggerated English accent.

"Should I be?"

"Of course. That's the whole idea."

"You specifically wanted me to come over and see you?"

Allison looked confused. "I don't think so."

"You say you wanted everyone to laugh, but you've painted tears falling down your cheeks. Why is that?"

"Smiling through my tears," she said airily. "In stories isn't the heroine always 'smiling through her tears'?"

"But why does the heroine have tears?"

"Because she thinks she's lost the man she loves, but then it turns out she hasn't." The giggling resumed.

"Have you lost the man you love?"

"No, but I know someone who has—Sally."

"Are you Sally?"

"That's hilarious."

"Mourning for Billy?"

Allison sobered abruptly. Her black-rimmed pale-green eyes narrowed. "She'll get over it. She's lucky he's dead. Whoever killed Billy did her a favor."

"If the tears on your face aren't for Billy, who are they for?"

"Mankind. Womankind. Everybody."

"And who's the big grin for?"

Allison shrugged. "Everybody."

"Even your mother?"

"Oh, Annemarie especially. She needs cheering up."

"But you didn't cheer her up, did you? What you called your artwork seems to have had the opposite effect."

"Win some, lose some."

"Have you got any cold cream? I'll help you get it off."

"If you want to."

"Then we'll talk about it on Wednesday. All right?"

"All right."

Dave couldn't interrogate Pete Hallberg until late Saturday afternoon, when Pete finished work. It was the kind of May day that suggests summer is closer than it really is. A deer-fly buzzed around Dave's head as he sat on the patio beside the Hallbergs' swimming pool.

"You were pretty good friends with Billy," Dave said.

"Yeah, I'm gonna miss him." Pete sprawled in the chair, his long legs staking out a triangle of territory.

"Constable Burns tells me that you and Billy used to shoot rats at the dump. What kind of gun did you use?"

"Sometimes I used my dad's .38. Other times I used an old .22 I've got."

"You must be a pretty good shot."

"I practice over at the Maywood Range."

"You a member of the Maywood Gun Club?"

"No, but Dad is."

"Do you happen to know anybody at the club who owns a Magnum or have you seen anyone use one for target shooting?"

Pete frowned. "There's a doctor-somebody who's got one. I think he's a dentist. The guys kid him about it. You know—like 'All those elephants and rhinoceroses in Maywood County better watch out.' That kind of thing. But he's the only one."

"Did you ever see Billy with a Magnum?"

Pete shifted in the chair, bringing his knees together. "That's right. His dad had one. But I never saw Billy with it."

"Would any of the boys working for your dad happen to have one?"

"No way. A Magnum isn't cheap."

"Was there anyone at school or at work who had it in for Billy?"

Pete shook his head, but with an air of uncertainty.

"Billy wasn't really popular, was he?"

"People didn't know him like I did. A lot of the guys were jealous—because of his looks and all the girls going for him."

"Did you ever hear anyone say he was going to get even with Billy for stealing his girl?"

"Sure, but what were they going to do? Beat him up and get busted? Anyway, nobody ever did."

"Could you give me the names of those classmates you heard threaten Billy?"

"I don't want to get anybody in trouble."

"It's just routine. I can easily get the names somewhere else."

Reluctantly, Pete gave Dave three names which Dave entered in his notebook. Disappointment in love was a classic motive for murder, but in every case Dave knew of, the disappointed lover had confronted his victim first before he killed him. Billy had been shot in the back of the head from thirty feet away. Quite possibly, Billy hadn't seen or heard the person who shot him.

"When was the last time you saw Billy?"

"That Friday. We went for lunch to Joe's Wagon for hamburgers."

"Did you see him after that?"

"No. He said he was going to skip his afternoon classes and go home, see if his check arrived."

"Did Billy tell you how he earned the money?"

"Sure. He acted in a movie. When he was down in Florida."

"Did he say what kind of movie?"

"Something educational. About health, he said."

"Had Billy ever acted in a movie before?"

"No, that was the first. Billy could have gone a long way. Mr. Craig said he was a natural."

"Did Mr. Craig ever say you could be an actor?"

"Me? Hell, no."

Dave rose. "Thanks for your help. Call the barracks if you hear about anything we should know."

He decided to stop at the barracks before returning to his apartment for a lonely Saturday night. He found two messages waiting for him. One, from Bannerman, said nothing useful had been discovered yet from the canvass of stores and homes on either side of Route 502, although two store owners had noticed Billy riding by on the new bike. The other, from Sam Burns, said Dave should call him at home. He dialed Sam's number.

"You find someone who picked Billy up?" he asked.

"No, but Bob Leahy, up the road from the gas station, saw Billy going toward the bank and wondered how come he wasn't in school."

"Looks like he didn't hitch a ride then."

"There's not too much traffic along those roads in the middle of the day."

"Anyone see Billy go up the road from the bank to the motorcycle dealer?"

"It's not all that far, but I'll ask around."

"Thanks."

Driving home, he had trouble keeping his eyes open, but by the time he let himself into his apartment, he felt restless and wakeful. He was too keyed up to study his Russian, and the semester exam was next week.

The bleak loneliness of the apartment didn't help. He needed someone to talk to, someone whose judgment he respected. He phoned Lucille on the slim chance she'd be home.

"Is something wrong?" she asked. The worry in her voice gave him a momentary joy. Maybe she still cared for him.

"Not exactly. It's just that I've been going at Billy's murder nonstop and I really need someone to argue with."

"I'm pretty good at that," Lucille said.

"Could you come over? We'll have a beer and pizza and knock this around."

"I've already eaten. And I honestly don't feel comfortable in your apartment, Dave." Her tone was mildly critical but not unkind. "Why don't you have something to eat and then come over here?"

"You're sure it's all right?"

"Of course. I'll expect you."

He knew Lucille didn't keep beer on hand, so he put a six-pack in the car. On the way to her house he stopped at Joe's Wagon for a hamburger, which he ate in the car, washed down with one of the beers.

She was wearing a long, loose paisley-print gown he hadn't seen before. He hadn't seen Lucille in at-home attire for two years. He'd been inside Lucille's cottage only once, right after she'd moved in. He'd brought over some things she'd left in the barn of the old house.

He took another can from the six-pack and put the rest in her refrigerator. Doing it gave him a friendly feeling of domesticity.

"What do you want to argue about?" she said with a smile.

"Colin, number one."

"You haven't found the gun, have you?"

"Not yet. But try this on. The S.A.'s office impounded Sam Durk's gun collection, which contained a Magnum. When they returned the collection to Mrs. Durk, the Magnum was missing. Sandra—you remember her—said she thought a cop had liberated it, but what if it got in Billy's hands somehow? Maybe he went up to the S.A.'s office and asked for it back and they gave it to him."

"Without making a record?"

"Slip-ups in paperwork aren't all that rare. Maybe he went over at lunch hour and showed whoever was there some kind of proof that he was the owner and he got away with it without signing anything."

"Too many holes in that script," Lucille said. "And where's the gun now?"

"It'll turn up."

Lucille sipped her white wine. "Do you really want to hear what I think?"

"Sure. That's why I'm here."

"I think Billy had some serious enemies—people who, for one reason or another, hated him enough to wish him dead. One of those enemies knew he would be going to the Conyac farm to show Colin his new motorcycle. The enemy waited for him in the woods by the old logging road, and when Billy turned in to the road and got off his motorcycle, he shot him. Then the killer simply walked away, taking the gun with him."

Dave rubbed his chin. "It could have happened that way, but how do we find this person?"

"What do we know about him?" Lucille had almost added "or her," but Allison was in enough trouble already without being added to Dave's list of suspects.

"He's a crack shot."

"And?"

"He owns or has access to a Magnum pistol."

"Would a gun like that be registered?"

"It should be. And there can't be all that many registered Magnums in Maywood County."

"If the killer lived in Maywood County. What if he was one of the New York people?"

"We could see if any of them had any guns registered in New York State."

Lucille counted on her fingers. "One, he's a crack shot. Two, he owns a fancy gun. And three, he had reason to hate Billy Durk. Any ideas there?"

"I spoke to one of Billy's friends at school and he gave me some names—kids who hated Billy because he stole their girlfriends. I'll put Harry on it Monday, but I don't hold out much hope." He sighed. "Billy might have seen and spoken to whoever killed him between the time he left his girlfriend Sally and the time he turned off 502 into the woods. There are a few minutes unaccounted for when he was outside McLeod's Highfields office, before he rode off. But that might not mean anything."

"Besides the three lovesick high-school boys, any other suspects?" Lucille asked.

"Not suspects. People we'll have to interrogate. Billy acted in some kind of health-education film when he and Sally were in Florida over spring vacation. There's something fishy about it, for a couple of reasons I'd better not go into." Among them, a check from a corporation in Ohio.

"But even if the movie was some kind of scam, I don't see how it would be a reason for murder, do you?"

"Unless Billy's acting was so terrible, somebody decided to put him out of his misery."

"Not funny," Dave said.

Why couldn't she stop herself from mocking him? Murder was a serious matter. What led her to respond to his legitimate gravity with mindless flippancy? "You're right," she said. "Besides, I can't picture Garrison Craig killing anybody. He was the director of the movie, wasn't he?"

Dave nodded. "What do you know about him?"

"Only the local gossip. He lives on Social Security and handouts. He rents that cottage from Sundergaard, who knew him in Hollywood in the good old days. Sundergaard lets him stay there for practically nothing, I've heard. And now and then Craig gets some star-struck young woman to share his bed and board. Usually a girl in her early twenties, plain-looking, ordinary, but bright, literate, in love with the theater. The parents call me. I can't tell them a girl needs therapy just because she's moved in with a man forty years older than she is. Hasn't Phil told you all this?"

"I haven't asked him. And I've got a few other people to see. But nothing fits together. Nothing feels right."

"Feels, Dave? I thought you relied on cold, pure logic." She exaggerated the raising of her eyebrows.

"That's a sexist remark." He wagged his finger at her. "These days men are allowed to have intuition, too. And my intuition tells me there's no way I can place Garrison Craig or the Farnols—the people Billy visited in Florida— at the scene of the murder. No way."

"But you do have other possible suspects—besides Colin."

"Long shots. Very long shots." He paused. "Sally

McLeod's a very frightened young lady. I suspect she knows more about Billy's murder than she's telling me."

"Even who did it?"

Dave nodded. "I'm going to have a talk with Marty Grunewald's stepdaughter, the girl you're seeing. I heard she was Sally's best friend."

"Do you have to?" She spoke without thinking, reacting instinctively to protect her patient.

"Any reason I shouldn't?"

"She's a very troubled girl."

"I'll go easy." He went into the kitchen to dispose of the beer can and get another.

Lucille watched him. She liked the way he moved—so purposefully, so sure of who he was. At that moment, all she could remember about their marriage was that it comforted her to have him near. The bitter arguments, the feeling of being constricted, shackled—all that had fled her memory. She smiled as he sat on the couch beside her.

"It feels good to be here," he said, with that slow gravity that made her want to laugh or cry. "I wish—"

He moved toward her, imploring her to respond. Instead, she stiffened. "I know what you wish," she said softly, "but it's too late."

CHAPTER

6

Sunday morning matched Dave's mood—a perfect day in May. When Sergeant Hillis called and proposed a round of golf at the Maywood Golf Club, Dave agreed. It would take his mind off the case. When he came back to it, he might have some fresh ideas about how to go about finding the murderer.

Hillis shot a 79 for the eighteen holes, playing way over his head. Dave was in trouble from the start—into the water, into the trees. By the fourteenth hole he stopped keeping score. He lost three golf balls.

The misery over his golf game effectively erased his misery over the unsolved murder. By Sunday afternoon, sitting in his apartment drinking beer and watching the PGA golfers go at it on television, he'd worked out a new scenario, based on the solid premise that Billy Durk was not a nice kid. After all, hadn't he let his brother take the rap for him for murder?

But what kind of meanness could he get into in a place like Maywood County? Drugs? Hookers? Bannerman had a line on whatever was going down in Maywood and Dave was sure Bannerman had questioned his informers about Billy. If he'd turned up anything, he would have told Dave.

Not drugs, then. Not prostitution. Extortion? The attitude in Maywood County was tolerant—live and let live as long as you didn't hurt anybody else. But maybe Billy had turned up a piece of information worth paying for.

The telephone number in Billy's pocket. Dave went to the phone and dialed Ellis Somers.

After Dave identified himself, Somers said, "I just learned this morning about Billy Durk. When I went to the market to get the Sunday paper. We got back last night from two weeks in the south of France. Are you calling about that?"

"Yes. I'd like to see you—as soon as possible."

Dave heard Somers's voice faintly, as if Somers had his hand over the receiver. "Is it all right?" The reply was inaudible. "We're not really unpacked yet," Somers said into the phone, "but you could come over, join us for cocktails. It's that time of day."

"Thanks. I'll be right there."

Somers lived in a small colonial farmhouse, nicely restored. The plantings around the house were spare in the colonial fashion and well cared for. In a room added on to the back of the house Somers and his friend sat in oak Morris chairs, tall drinks on the table between them.

Somers introduced Dave to Perry, "better known as Cher because he's really such a dear." Somers sent Perry to fetch Dave a vodka and tonic "in honor of the month of May or whatever." When Perry had delivered the drink, Somers said to him, "Wouldn't now be a good time to start dinner?" Perry nodded and departed, taking his drink with him.

"Now what is it you'd like to know?" Somers said. His

Gloucester Library
P.O. Box 2380
Gloucester, VA 23061

hair was brown, short and tightly curled, without a trace of gray, his skin deeply tanned, and his slim body boyish, but his manner was that of an older man used to giving orders and being obeyed.

"When did you leave for Europe?" Dave asked.

"Two weeks ago yesterday—early Saturday morning. But we left Highfields the day before—Friday—and spent the night at a friend's apartment in New York."

"What time did you leave Highfields?"

"After lunch."

"Did you drive in?"

"Yes, we parked in the apartment garage."

"You arrived at your friend's apartment when?"

"At ten minutes to four. My friend has a handsome clock in his foyer and I noted the time"

"You of course know when Billy was murdered," Dave said.

"Not exactly. Around the end of April, wasn't it? About two weeks ago? That's what I heard at the market. I haven't had a chance yet to read the papers."

"It was two weeks ago Friday." Dave found Somers's answers a shade too smooth. And Somers hadn't seemed one bit surprised at Dave's interrogation. "What do you think of Billy Durk?" he asked.

"I didn't like him"

"Was it a general dislike or did you have a personal reason to dislike him?"

"I'd say it was both. He was an evil little bastard." He spoke without emotion, as if describing an object rather than a person.

"What was your personal reason?"

"He tried to hustle me." Somers snorted. "He picked the wrong party—in both senses."

"How exactly?"

"He crashed a big party I had here around the middle of March. He came on to just about everybody with his innocent farm-boy act. I would have sent him home, but it was kind of amusing. We tried to guess what movie star he was impersonating. Harmless. But two days after the party our innocent farm boy stopped by after school and made me a proposition I couldn't afford to turn down." Somers laughed mirthlessly. "He said that unless I gave him five thousand dollars, he was going to tell the police that I and my guests had tried to gang-rape him. Beautiful, no?"

"How did you respond?"

"I told him I'd been out of the closet for years and so had most of my guests. And most of us were much too old for orgies. I also informed pretty Billy that since extortion was illegal, I would be on the phone to the police if he didn't get himself off my property in the next ten seconds."

"Did he leave?"

"Oh yes. Shuffling his feet and giving me a mean look with those sexy eyes. Then I began to wonder if I hadn't been foolish. I wasn't worried about the extortion but about what he might do out of spite. He killed his father, didn't he? Five thousand isn't too much to pay to keep alive. I really had the shakes for days afterward."

"Did you hear from him again?"

"No."

"You're sure? Not even a phone call?"

"No."

"You admit he frightened you."

"Yes. I think he frightened a lot of people."

"But you didn't tell us."

Somers sighed. "Maybe I should have. Especially now that somebody's killed him. Saved me the trouble."

"Could you give me your friend's name in New York and the address of his apartment?"

"His name is Petrakis, but he wasn't there. The door-man gave me the key. You can ask the doorman at 731 East Fifty-ninth Street."

Dave made a note of the name and address. He would have to check Somers's alibi with the doorman and the garage attendant.

He thanked Somers for his cooperation and, outside the house, noted the license number of the black BMW in the driveway. He now at last had someone besides Colin with both motive and opportunity.

The Monday morning *Times Democrat* carried the ban-ner headline: COLIN CONFESSED, BOY SAYS. The story read:

> Colin Durk, convicted of killing his father, allegedly told a friend at the Connecticut Youth Academy that he had also killed his brother Billy. According to State Police spokesman Arnold Wollman, the youth over-heard Colin say to another inmate: "Sure I killed him. I didn't want him around when I got out."
>
> Colin Durk's brother disappeared April 20. The body of Billy Durk was discovered on Youth Academy property a week later, on April 27. Although the murder weapon has not been located, the State's At-torney is preparing to indict Colin Durk for murder of his brother.

As soon as he arrived at the barracks, Dave asked Phil to get Sandra Murphy on the phone. While he waited and attempted to quiet his rage, he remembered that he had neglected to return reporters' calls in the week just past. But what could he have said to them?

"What the hell does the MCU think they're doing?" he asked Sandra.

"I just this minute saw the paper," she said. "I'll have to talk to them, find out who authorized Wollman to talk."

"You told me last week your investigators hadn't turned up anything."

"They hadn't. Until Friday. The informant called one of the Unit detectives and told him what he had overheard. The boy hadn't spoken up while the men were at Conyac because he feared retaliation. They're over at Conyac now, checking his story."

"The newspaper says you're preparing to indict."

"We're preparing to bring him in. Whether we indict depends on what he says."

"You're making a serious mistake, concentrating all your attention on Colin and Conyac."

"Really? What makes you say that?"

"I've got a couple of other roads I'm looking down."

"Shouldn't we know about them?"

"You and the MCU do your thing and I'll do mine. The only difference is that I'll keep what I'm doing out of the newspapers."

"Want to bet?" Sandra was laughing as she hung up.

Phil's follow-up call to the Ohio Secretary of State revealed that the corporate directors of Columbus Educational Enterprises were Harold Davenport, Martha Davenport, and Operita Strawbridge. The Davenports resided in Columbus, Ohio. Ms. Strawbridge resided in Key Doro, Florida.

Dave asked Phil to keep trying the Farnols' number until he got an answer. With luck Dave would be able to interrogate the Farnols the next day, Tuesday, when he'd be going into New York City to check Ellis Somers's alibi.

Harry was at Maywood High, interrogating the three boys Pete Hallberg had named. He returned to the barracks at noon.

———

"Find anything?" Dave asked him.

"Nothing beyond corroboration that Billy had threatened to kill his brother when Colin got out of Conyac."

"Did any of the boys say why Billy wanted to kill his brother?"

"Sure. Because otherwise Colin was going to kill him. In fact, Billy told one of the boys, 'If I'm killed, remember it's Colin who did it.'"

"Did the boy believe him?"

"No. He thought Billy was lying, trying to make Colin out to be a psycho killer when practically everyone in Highfields knew it was Billy who shot their father."

"That fits," Dave said.

Shortly after lunch Phil reached the Farnols. Mr. Farnol said he and his wife would welcome the opportunity to discuss Billy Durk with Lieutenant Littlejohn. They would be in their apartment at three the following afternoon.

Dave called the Grunewalds. Annemarie answered the phone.

"I'd like to come by and have a little chat with Allison after school today," Dave said.

"Is this absolutely necessary?"

"I'm afraid so."

"I'll warn her."

Dave had never been inside the Grunewald house. The conventional Early American furniture surprised him. On the walls of the living room hung oil portraits of Allison and Marty Grunewald and a self-portrait of Annemarie. The famous depictions of cows in haunted light were nowhere to be seen.

"Can I get you coffee or a beer?" Annemarie asked.

"No, thanks."

"Allison will be down in a minute."

The girl appeared almost as soon as Annemarie left the

room. "Hello, Lieutenant," she said. "I doubt I can help you, but fire away." She sat primly, her hands clasped over one knee. Her attitude made him feel absurdly intrusive.

"Can you tell me first where you were Friday afternoon two weeks ago?"

"I was in school until ten minutes of three. Then I came home. I have my own car."

"Did you come straight home?"

Was there a moment's hesitation?

"Yes. Of course."

"On your way home from Maywood High, did you see Billy Durk?"

"No."

"Did you leave home anytime Friday afternoon or evening?"

"No."

"I understand you were tutoring Billy up until spring vacation. Then after he returned from his trip to Florida, you stopped. Could you tell me why?"

"It was wasted effort. He wasn't serious about graduating."

"Didn't your friend Sally McLeod continue the tutoring?"

"If you can call it that."

"You sound as if you didn't approve of Sally's relationship with Billy. Is that correct?"

"He was out to destroy her. If he hadn't been killed, he would have done it—completely."

"How destroy? Could you be more specific?"

Again the hesitation. "He enslaved her. He got her to do—unspeakable things."

"Such as?"

Allison shook her head.

"Did Sally tell you about these unspeakable acts?"

107

"No. Of course not."

"Then how did you come to know about them?"

Allison stared at him. "I knew, that's all."

"But how? Who told you?"

Her eyes narrowed. "Billy." She made the name sound like a curse.

"Why would he tell you such things? Was he boasting? Trying to disgust you?"

"Both."

"Could he have been lying?"

"What difference would that make? He was evil through and through."

"Let's say he was lying. Why would he tell such things to you?"

"He knew I detested him. He treated it like a big joke—what he'd done to Sally."

"I wish you could be more specific." Dave sat back, prepared to wait as long as necessary for an answer.

But after a few minutes Allison said, "I'm sorry. I can't talk about it."

Dave gave her a stern look. "You know, don't you, that it's illegal to withhold information that might help in solving a crime."

Allison laughed lightly. "Would you put me in jail? That would be interesting."

"No one's going to put you in jail, Allison. We just need all the help we can get to find out who killed Billy Durk. If we don't get some answers soon, there's a good chance the state will pin it on Colin."

"What's wrong with that?" she said coolly. "He's still under age. He'd get another year at Conyac. So what?"

"It would be a lot worse. He'd be tried as an adult, even if he is only fifteen. If he committed the murder, he did it while he was in custody, on state property. No judge would recommend leniency under those circumstances."

Allison shrugged. "Too bad then about Colin. He's one of life's victims."

"Like your friend Sally?"

"I don't know why you keep calling her my friend. She's not. I don't have any friends."

The sudden pallor of her skin warned him he should go no further. "I wish you'd think of me as a friend," he said, rising. "I hope you'll decide before it's too late to tell me what you couldn't tell me today."

Her response was a bright and empty smile. "You must be kidding," she said.

The interview, despite its depressing conclusion, confirmed Dave's suspicion that there were a number of people with strong reasons to want Billy Durk dead. He returned to the barracks. Harry had questioned Tess Sandford. She'd seen no one speaking to Billy Durk outside McLeod's Highfields office on Friday, April 20. Harry had also heard from New York State. No guns were registered in the name of Dane or Margery Farnol.

"I double-checked with Santini at MCU. No firearms registered for Somers," Harry reported. "None for McLeod, Grunewald, Echinger—that's Mrs. Grunewald— or Garrison Craig. Actually, none registered for Sam Durk. You remember when we checked last year. He never registered any one of those guns in his collection." Harry grunted. "Farmers don't recognize a law that interferes with a man's right to protect his property."

Dave nodded wearily. "I don't suppose the missing Magnum has turned up in the S.A.'s office either."

"It hasn't. Find out anything from Grunewald's stepdaughter?"

"She knows something, but I don't know how I'm going to dig it out."

"The McLeods check out. Mrs. McLeod was playing bridge like you said, and Mrs. Olin told me they were buying the Davis place."

Dave sighed. News of the Olins' purchase would be all over Highfields by evening.

He asked Phil to get him Bannerman. "Any luck?" he asked Maywood's chief of police.

"I got three more people reported seeing Billy on the bike on 502. One report of a large new car parked on the side of the highway just west of the logging road. A woman who'd just moved to Maywood and happened to be going east on 502. She's interested in undeveloped property and that's why she noticed the Conyac woods right in the middle of all the commercial development on 502. But she couldn't say what make the car was or what color. Just that it was big and looked new. It might mean something or nothing at all."

"I've got a couple more I'd like your men to ask about," Dave said. "A dark green '76 Mustang, belonging to Allison Friely, Marty Grunewald's stepdaughter, going east or west on 502 that afternoon. And a black '84 BMW— same time, same directions, belonging to Ellis Somers. Both Highfields residents, Connecticut plates."

"Got it," Bannerman said.

Dave put down the phone and told Harry the gist of Bannerman's report.

Harry stood with his arms crossed over his chest. "The longer it takes—"

"I know."

"A few more days and nobody will remember anything."

"Go home, will you?" Dave bent over the blank sheet

of lined paper. He was about to make a list of suspects and questions regarding each that remained to be answered when Phil buzzed.

"Garrison Craig is here. Can you see him?"

"Send him in."

Craig filled the door to Dave's office. His white hair, swept back from a wide forehead, almost reached his shoulders. "I just got in from the Coast," Craig said with a broad smile. "I understand you wanted to see me."

"Have a seat."

Craig was barely able to squeeze himself into the oak chair. His fleshy thighs extruded between the chair's slats. "I assume you'd like to know where I was the afternoon Billy Durk was murdered."

Dave nodded. "That's a start."

"I was in the cutting room of Amphitryon Video, editing video tape. Amphitryon Video is located at 2133 La Cienega Boulevard, in L.A. Phone number 313-771-0301." Craig's faded blue eyes registered amusement as he watched Dave write the information he'd given him. Despite his white hair and sagging jowls, his manner was that of a bright and prankish adolescent.

"Thanks," Dave said. He matched Craig's mocking grin. "And of course you wouldn't be telling me this if it wasn't going to check out."

"Of course. And there's maybe fifty people who saw me that day in L.A. Even if I took the Red-eye the night before, I wouldn't have had time to get to Highfields from JFK, shoot Billy, get back to JFK and back to L.A. the same day. Right?"

"Right." Dave eyed Craig. "Why did you think we'd suspect you of killing Billy?"

Craig shifted uncomfortably. "Everybody told me you were looking for me. If that wasn't the reason, what was?

It's a damn shame. Billy could have developed into a big star—with the proper guidance."

"Relax," Dave said. "You're not a suspect. But Billy's murder may be connected in some way with the video you made in Florida. I'm told the video covered some aspect of health education. Is that right?"

"Yes. After the initial airing on cable, the cassette will be distributed to health professionals."

Craig's abrupt switch to a businesslike tone was disconcerting. "What sort of health professionals?" Dave asked.

"Primarily sex therapists. The video gives instruction in the alleviation of certain sexual dysfunctions. It will be accompanied by a manual written by a recognized authority in the field of sex therapy."

"In other words," Dave said, "a blue movie."

Craig looked offended. "Absolutely not."

"Could I see a copy of the tape?"

"It's still being edited. I'll be happy to give you a cassette with my compliments, when it's ready."

"When will that be?"

"About six months."

"I'm not sure you understand, Mr. Craig. This is a police matter. I have to see that tape right now."

"That's not possible."

Dave eyed him sternly. "You're not telling me it's impossible to make copies of the tape the California company is working on."

"They won't release the tape to anybody, not even me."

"Why not?"

Craig cleared his throat. "I owe them money."

"That's your problem." Dave made a mental note to

ask Farnol how much money he'd given Craig. "The L.A. police will know what to do."

Craig looked at him in alarm. "They can't confiscate it. It's not obscene or pornographic. It's educational. It's protected by the First Amendment. I'll sue the police if—" Craig's fleshy jowls quivered.

"I'm not talking about confiscation or seizure. I only want to see a copy, see if there's anything there to lead me to Billy's murderer." He paused and eyed Craig with a touch of sympathy. "Who's in the movie—besides Billy?"

"My friend Dorry—ex-friend, I should say. She decided to stay in L.A.—with a surfer, healthy young animal. Oh well, at my age—" His laugh indicated that Dorry was not irreplaceable.

"Anybody else?"

"Billy's friend Sally. I don't remember her last name but I hear her grandfather's a big shot in real estate."

"You mean to say you've never run into Andy McLeod in all your years here in Highfields?"

"No. Should I have?" The widening of his faded blue eyes increased Dave's certainty that Craig was lying.

"Anybody else in the movie? Billy the only male?"

"Yes." Craig wet his lips. "He was quite sufficient for our purposes."

Dave ignored the suggestive titter. "How did Farnol pay you—cash or check?"

"Well—both."

"Did the checks come from a company in Ohio?"

"Yes, as a matter of fact."

"Do you know how the Ohio company relates to Farnol?"

"No, I don't. Farnol has business interests all over the world. He made his first million before he was thirty."

113

"Can you think of anybody who might have killed Billy?"

Craig wrinkled his broad, pale brow. "What about some kid at Maywood High? Maybe Billy stole his girl."

"Any other ideas?"

Craig shook his head. "Sorry."

"Do you own a gun?"

"Good God, no!"

"Do you know Ellis Somers?"

"Who doesn't?"

"Might Somers have had a reason to kill Billy?"

"Billy might have tried to pull a fast one on old Ellis. Shake him down. I wouldn't put it past him. But I can't visualize Ellis with a gun in his hand. Completely out of character."

"Did Billy happen to mention any threats on his life while you were in Florida?"

"He said his brother Colin might try to kill him once he got out of jail, but Billy laughed about it. I didn't get the impression it was a serious possibility."

Dave rose from his desk. "Thanks for coming in. I hope you're not planning to do any more traveling for the next couple of weeks."

"No." Craig lumbered to his feet and held out his hand. "If you have any more questions, you'll find me at home."

"Fine."

When Craig had left, Dave stood at the window and watched cars passing on the ridge above the barracks. It was raining again, washing away more of the farmers' seed. Just below the ridge there was a sharp curve in the highway. He heard the squeal of brakes on the wet road. It was a sure bet there'd be another overturned car there before the day was over.

114

At last he had the answer to one important question. The unspeakable thing Billy had forced Sally to do was to appear in a sex flick, to perform sexually with Billy and possibly the girl Dorry before Craig, a cameraman, and who knew how many others. Would Farnol have watched, too?

Now he knew Sally's secret. And she was terrified it might be disclosed. Did Sally know that Billy had told her secret to Allison? Might that disclosure have frightened and angered Sally enough to leave the real-estate office that Friday afternoon, follow her lover down the highway, and when he turned into the logging road, come up behind him and shoot him? Or might Allison, to keep Billy from hurting her friend Sally further, have been the one to silence him forever?

Dave asked Harry to double-check Sally McLeod's alibi. How long had she remained at the real-estate office? When had she arrived home at Windrush Farm? If Harry turned up any gaps, Dave would have to see Sally once more. If there were no gaps, he'd have another go at Allison.

Before leaving the barracks, Dave called Santini at MCU headquarters and asked him to take whatever steps were necessary to secure a copy of a videotape produced by Garrison Craig and being held by Amphitryon Video at 2133 La Cienega Boulevard in Los Angeles. "They won't release it to Craig because he owes them," Dave explained.

"Why do you need to see it?" Santini said.

"It's a sex flick. Starring Billy Durk and his girlfriend Sally McLeod. Depending on how steamy it is, it might give us a motive for murder."

"Listen, don't waste our time. Colin did it and we can prove it."

"How?"

"That kid said he admitted it."

"The kid might be brown-nosing you. You haven't got confirmation, have you?"

"We'll get it. We're that close."

"I'd still like to see that tape," Dave said.

"I'll have to get a court order. It might take a couple of weeks."

"You can do better than that. It wouldn't look so good if the newspapers decided you were railroading Colin."

"I'll try to speed it up," Santini said.

"Thanks."

Dave wondered if he would get the videotape soon enough to be of any use.

Tuesday Dave started for New York after nine to avoid rush-hour traffic. He pulled up in front of 731 East 59th Street shortly before eleven.

He showed the doorman his badge. "Do you remember giving a man named Ellis Somers the key to Mr. Petrakis's apartment two weeks ago last Friday?"

"Did he have a friend along? A young blond guy? Gay?" The doorman asked.

"That's right."

"Petrakis has a lot of friends like that. But he's all right."

"About what time of day was it when you gave Mr. Somers the key?"

"Let me think. I go off at five. He must have come in about an hour before, around four o'clock."

"Thanks." Dave walked down the ramp into the garage. He rapped on the ticket window to get the attendant's attention. "Are you here on Friday afternoons?" he asked, showing his badge.

The man nodded.

"Two weeks ago Friday did you check in a black '84 BMW, Connecticut license plate UX 6112?"

"Give me a minute. I'll look at the tickets." The attendant reached under the high shelf and brought out a box crammed with tickets. "If it was more than a month, I wouldn't have it," he said. He riffled through the tickets. "Here it is. Friday, April 20, checked in 3:46 P.M., out Saturday, April 21, 7:04 A.M. That do it?"

"Just fine. Many thanks."

Cross off Ellis Somers.

Dave parked his car on the street and walked west to the Museum of Modern Art. He had time to kill until his appointment with the Farnols, and the museum was a great place to kill time. One of the college courses he'd taken was Art Appreciation. He'd come away from the course with a pretty good understanding of what modern artists were trying to do. He especially liked to look at the new wrinkles on old themes that the newest artists had been exploring. Maybe because they'd run out of fresh ideas? Anyway, he enjoyed it.

Besides the pictures, he liked to look at the young women passing through the galleries. They seemed so serious, so smart and purposeful—like Lucille. You could say they were his type. Since the divorce he'd had brief affairs with three women he'd met at MOMA. He started the conversation with each of them the same way: "I noticed you admiring the Schnabel (or whatever). What do you see in it? Maybe because I'm a cop—a Connecticut Trooper, actually—I don't look at it right."

His being a cop interested in modern art always surprised and intrigued these women. It was easy to take it from there.

Too easy. After a few weeks he started to wish the

woman were Lucille, and his initial attraction to her dwindled away to nothing. Despite his often painful loneliness, it was a game he'd lost interest in playing.

He arrived at the Farnols' door on the dot of three. Farnol led him into a vast living room. Windows on two walls overlooked the East River and gave a view of the Chrysler and Empire State Buildings to the south.

"On a clear day you can see the World Trade towers," Farnol said.

Mrs. Farnol rose to greet him. She was a crisp-featured blonde, an inch or two taller than her husband, with a trim athletic figure. "Please call me Marge," she said. She rang a small glass bell on a glass coffee table that fronted a long white couch. Except for circles of peach color in the thick white carpet and peach-colored begonias blooming in pots in a corner arrangement between the wide windows, everything in the room was white.

"We were just going to have tea," Farnol said. "Or would you like something stronger?"

"Tea will be fine." Dave sat in a white leather and chromium chair. A young Japanese brought in the tea tray and Marge Farnol made a ceremony of pouring. "We're nuts about anything Japanese," she said.

"Well, how can we help you?" Farnol sat at the other end of the couch from his wife. His tanned youthful face and crewcut gray hair conformed agreeably to Dave's mental picture of the successful young entrepreneur.

"I understand," Dave began, "that you have business interests all over the world."

"That's right. Korea, Hong Kong, Mexico. You were lucky to catch us in New York. We just got in Sunday night from Brazil."

"Does your company manufacture computers in all

these places?" Dave wasn't sure he'd worded the question correctly.

"I don't have one company," Farnol said. "I have several. The only company that makes computers is the one in Mexico. I'm into a lot of different things—lasers, bio-engineering, cable TV, whatever I think can eventually turn a profit. I'm what's called a venture capitalist." His grin countered any suggestion of boastfulness.

"How did Garrison Craig fit in?"

"Not one of my better judgments." Farnol looked toward his wife, who shook her head ruefully. "But Craig came to me with what sounded like a good proposition. You know that one of the problems with cable is finding enough programs at reasonable cost. Craig had the credentials from shooting B and C pictures in the past, and he brought me this script he must have had sitting on a shelf somewhere— a rewrite of *The Blue Lagoon* he was going to shoot with a couple of amateurs like cinéma vérité and bring in for under a hundred grand. I thought, what's to lose? We could use my Key Doro house and beach for location shots, and we hired a couple of Miami cameramen who'd been shooting TV commercials. I met the so-called actors at a party at Craig's and the boy certainly looked right. His girlfriend wasn't too bad either. I figured Craig would know how to get a performance out of them." He sighed. "You sure you want to hear all this?"

"Very much," Dave said.

"You could see at the end of the first week it wasn't going to work."

"The tapes were awful," Mrs. Farnol said.

"Those poor kids. They moved like wind-up soldiers and only Craig's fat girlfriend could speak a line so you could understand what she was saying. So then Craig had a brainstorm. Shoot it as soft porn, no dialogue, just a voice-over which Craig would do, pretending it was a health-education film. I thought the idea was pretty sick, but if it kept the venture from being a total loss, I'd go along with it." Another sigh and twisted grin. "Wrong again."

"It wasn't sexy enough or what?" Dave asked.

"Sexy! You could use it to cure insomnia."

"Of course," Marge Farnol said, "Craig insisted it would be just nifty after editing."

"Craig suckered me twice." Momentarily Farnol allowed his anger to be revealed. "A third time? No way."

"So you wouldn't pay for the tapes to be edited or duplicated," Dave said.

"Correct."

"And you gave Craig no more money?"

"Ditto."

"Do you mind telling me how much you paid Craig in toto?"

"Not at all. It was five grand up front and five grand to send him on his way. He was supposed to get another ten grand when the tape was finished."

"Who paid Craig's way to California?"

"He must have had some money left from what I paid him in Florida."

"He and Billy were paid through your Ohio corporation, I noticed. The principals of the corporation are two people named Davenport and somebody named Operita Strawbridge. Who are they?"

"The Davenports are my parents," Marge Farnol said.

"And Operita works for us in Florida," Dane Farnol said.

"So it's kind of a dummy corporation?"

Farnol shrugged. "It's convenient for disbursements when a venture is in its beginning stages. I don't use it for anything else."

"A dummy corporation is also useful for laundering money." Dave watched Farnol's reaction. It told him nothing.

"I've never been attracted to drugs," Farnol said coolly. "I average thirty percent on my money legitimately and that's plenty for anybody."

Smooth, Dave thought. "When Billy Durk was in Florida or afterward, did he try to shake you down?"

Both Mr. and Mrs. Farnol were taken off guard by the question. "What makes you ask?" Farnol said, a slight tremor in his voice.

"As far as I can tell, Billy tried to shake down anybody he thought had money. How'd he work it on you?"

The Farnols exchanged worried looks. Mrs. Farnol nodded and her husband chewed his lip before answering. "The little bastard said he was going to get us on the Mann Act—transporting a young woman across state lines for obscene purposes. It was while we were on my plane going to New York. I said I'd get back to him. I left him with the impression that I'd pay him something to keep him quiet. Then, the minute we landed, I called my lawyer and he told me not to worry. In fact, if I wanted, I could get Billy for attempted extortion. But I figured why bother? We left two days later for São Paulo and while we were there my lawyer phoned to tell me about the murder."

So Farnol had an ironclad alibi, Dave thought, but Farnol also had the money and the contacts to contract out Billy's murder if that's what he decided to do. "How much was Billy asking?"

"Only four thousand—above the one thousand I was paying him and his girl for their so-called acting."

Not worth killing him for, Dave thought. Billy's attempts at extortion had gone nowhere. Or had they?

Maybe Billy had finally scored with the person who murdered him.

"Did you ever hear Billy say anything about having enemies? Or being afraid of someone?"

"To tell you the truth, I never had a conversation with him till we were on the plane. I don't think Marge ever talked to him either." Farnol looked questioningly toward his wife.

"There was one time," she said. "I told you about it, Dane." She turned to Dave. "Billy came up to me one afternoon when I was sunning on the beach. He shuffled his feet in the sand for a few minutes, then said right out, without preamble, 'Did you ever hire a gigolo, Mrs. Farnol? Like they talk about in that movie *Midnight Cowboy?*' I had to put my hand over my mouth to keep from laughing. Was he planning to offer me his services? Did I look as if I needed him?" She gave a self-conscious laugh. "Anyway, I said no, and he ran off without another word."

Dave saw no reason to doubt her story. It fitted his picture of Billy as an explosive combination of naïveté and sophistication. "Do you own a gun, Mr. Farnol?" he asked.

"Not exactly. Mrs. Strawbridge, who stays in the Key Doro house year-round, asked me to get one for her, so I did. It's registered in my name in Florida."

"What kind of gun is it?"

"I don't know. I went to a store in Miami and asked for something my housekeeper could use for protection."

"Does the gun have a long barrel?" With his hands he indicated the six-inch length of the Magnum's barrel. "About like this?"

"No. Shorter. As I remember it, it's not a very big gun. I haven't seen it in a couple of years."

Dave rose. "I want to thank you for your cooperation.

If I need to get back in touch, is there a number I can call where I could be sure to reach you?"

"Just a second, I'll give you my card." Farnol reached into the drawer of a small ornamental desk standing against the wall leading into the foyer and took out a business card, which he handed to Dave. "That's my central office—only three people. I call in at least once a day no matter where I am."

"Thanks again." Dave pocketed the card.

Driving back to Highfields, Dave wondered if he would ever stop running into dead ends. Except for the trip to the museum, the whole day in New York had been fruitless. Of course, he'd have to check Farnol's gun with the Florida authorities, but he had not a scintilla of hope that it would turn out to be the murder weapon.

CHAPTER

7

Shortly before her session with Allison, Lucille received a phone call from Simon Dennis, the psychologist at Conyac. He sounded frantic. "They've taken Colin and put him in the County jail."

"Who is they?"

"The Major Crime Unit detectives. They did an end run on me and Hal Rubin, our lawyer. Protecting the state's citizens is what they call it."

"And you're afraid they'll get Colin to confess even if he didn't do it?"

"I'm positive that's what they're up to. And they'll succeed. Colin has no reason to expect justice to prevail, and he has every reason to buckle under to the voice of authority. He'll give them what they want."

"What can I do?"

"Call Dave. I'd call him myself, but I get the impression he doesn't like me, and besides, it would look like I'm trying to cover my hind end here at Conyac."

"Wouldn't MCU or the S.A.'s office have told Dave that they were taking Colin in?"

"They're supposed to, but I'm pretty sure they didn't. I got the impression they think Dave is biased in Colin's favor simply because he doubts Colin was the murderer."

"I'll call him as soon as I'm finished with my next patient."

Lucille leaned back in her chair, closed her eyes, and began her relaxation routine. Somehow she had to get control over the conflicting emotions Allison aroused in her. In truth, she dreaded the session about to begin. Dave had seen Allison on Monday, and Allison's behavior the previous Friday night indicated that the girl was critically near the breaking point. At the same time, Lucille suspected— she did not *know*—that Allison's increasingly troubled behavior was related to Billy's murder. Lucille suspected— she did not *know*—that Allison knew the identity of the murderer. Now, with Colin's arrest, it was vital that she get Allison to reveal what she was hiding.

The girl entered her office looking as poised and untroubled as she had on her first visit. "Isn't it a beautiful day?" Allison said, sitting on the couch.

"Yes, it is." Lucille decided to remain behind her desk. She needed all the air of authority she could muster. She needed, above all, to maintain a psychic distance from Allison, because in order to unearth Allison's secret, cold persistence might be necessary.

"I'm really sorry you had to make a house call Friday night. I don't know why Annemarie got so hysterical. Will you forgive me?"

"There's nothing to forgive." Her voice was stern, without softness or sympathy. "You're not stupid, Allison. You must know why your mother is so worried about you."

Allison grinned impishly. "Maybe I do, maybe I don't. Why do you sound so angry?"

"Because I don't think you've been straight with me. It's natural to repress painful memories, like rape, but I think you've chosen to withhold information about the last few months, not because it would be painful to talk about, but, well, for other reasons. And I suspect that the information you've withheld is connected with the behavior that so worries your mother."

Allison, avoiding Lucille's challenging gaze, looked toward the door. "What if it is?"

"Wouldn't it help to talk about it? What passes between us in this room is confidential."

"No, it isn't. You told Lieutenant Littlejohn about Billy's threat to kill Colin."

"Yes, because the doctor-patient privilege doesn't extend to knowledge of an impending crime. Also, as you must know, you weren't the only one to hear Billy make that threat." Lucille folded her hands over the notepad on her desk. "Are you trying to tell me that the information you're withholding is related to Billy's murder and that I wouldn't be allowed to keep it confidential?"

Allison sat stiffly erect. She said nothing.

"Would you be more willing to talk if I told you that Colin has been arrested by the state investigators and they're probably going to get him to confess?"

"Oh no!" Her hand flew to her lips. "What should I do?"

"You know the answer," Lucille said, again without sympathy.

"I can't! Too many people have been hurt already."

"By Billy?"

"Yes."

"Tell me who Billy has hurt. Besides yourself and Sally."

"Colin."

"He's continuing to hurt his brother, even after his own death. Isn't he?"

Allison stared at her. "The evil goes on and on. First his father, maybe his grandfather—his father was a terrible man."

Lucille nodded. "Are you trying to say that Billy wasn't responsible for the bad he did?"

"I don't know. I just don't know." Allison crossed her arms over her breasts. "Who puts evil into the world? Is it Satan? Do you believe in the devil?"

"No. Nor in witches or the bad seed or damnation. I think it's what happens here on earth, in someone's lifetime, especially during childhood, that determines how that person is going to behave, for good or ill."

Allison smiled strangely. "I suppose that's what you have to believe in your business." The strange smile lingered. "But no psychotherapist could have stopped Billy. He would have gone on and on, hurting more and more people. The only way to stop him was to kill him." She paused. "I've thought about it. It's like a poisoned lake. The water may have been pure and clean once, but somehow it was poisoned—it doesn't really matter where the poison came from. And now nothing grows in the lake—no fish, no algae, nothing. And when the water spills over the banks, it kills the weeds and the flowers and the grass, too. It kills everything it touches. You have to get rid of the poison in the water if you want anything to grow there again."

Was Allison trying to tell her she was the one who had cleansed the lake of its poison? And if she pushed further and Allison confessed to the murder, Lucille would have to tell Dave, wouldn't she? But first she'd have to establish that Allison was indeed telling the truth, not fantasizing. And while she worked at that, what about Colin? "That's an interesting analogy," she said. "I wonder what kind of instrument you'd use to get poison out. Would you use a gun?"

"Of course not."

"But it was a gun that killed Billy." She gave Allison time to digest the statement. "Do you know anything about the gun that killed Billy? Did it belong to your stepfather?"

The girl shook her head. "I don't know. I told you I don't know."

"What kind of gun does your stepfather own?"

"It's an old police gun." She put her hand to her eyes, shading them. "That's what Marty says it is. I've never seen it."

Was there a shade too much innocence in her reply? "Have you ever fired a gun?"

"Ugh!" Allison wrinkled her nose, then gave Lucille a shrewd look. "Why are you asking me these questions? You're not supposed to be a detective."

Lucille met the girl's accusatory gaze. "I thought we both agreed that your depression arose, at least in part, from your experiences with Billy Durk, both in the past and recently. And that because of your feelings about Billy, you might consider yourself guilty of his murder, whether you actually had anything to do with it or not. Am I wrong?"

Allison continued to stare at her.

"Further, I think we've pretty well established that you do know something about the murder, which you refuse to disclose, and that this knowledge has been almost unbearably stressful."

The girl sat motionless. Her stare neither confirmed nor denied Lucille's supposition.

"When you feel ready to tell me about it, I'm ready to listen." She leaned back in her desk chair. They sat for several minutes in silence.

"Do you want to hear how he happened to rape me?" Allison said finally, in a dry voice.

"I'd like to." Lucille rounded her desk and sat in the straight chair opposite the couch. She'd gone as far as she dared with toughness. Now, once again, it was important to show Allison sympathy and acceptance.

"It was right after we first came to Highfields," Allison began. "I was fourteen and Billy was fifteen. Annemarie and I had already met all of Marty's relatives. I was pretty silly then, kind of boy-crazy, the way fourteen-year-old girls are. And Billy, you know, was very handsome. All the girls at Maywood High were goofy about him. Me, too." Allison's tone remained unemotional. "Anyway, one Saturday evening when Marty and Annemarie were at a party, who should knock on the door but Billy, come to hear my old Beatle records, he said. So like a dope I asked him up to my room where I have my stereo, and I started to play the records. He took a joint—marijuana—"

"I know," Lucille said.

"—from his pocket, and we shared it while we listened to the records. I'd had marijuana once before, in junior high, but that time it didn't do anything. This time I was floating. You know, I was floating to begin with, there alone with the boy every girl in school was nuts about, and he had his arm around me, and I felt—just wonderful." Allison's hands were clasped, the knuckles white. "Then, all of a sudden, he was all over me. I told him I was a virgin, but he just wouldn't let me go. Then when I managed to break free, he knocked me down and I hit my head on the open door. I told Annemarie I'd bumped into the door to explain the egg on my forehead." Allison nodded solemnly. "You see, I never lie to my mother."

"That was sad, wasn't it, not being able to tell your mother what really happened," Lucille said.

"I suppose so, but I didn't want to queer things for her with Marty. And I loved Highfields. Besides, I thought it was my own fault for being such a dope, asking Billy to my room, smoking the joint."

"You blamed yourself for being raped?"

"Pretty sick, isn't it? I mean, he was brutal. He wouldn't let me up. He pinned my arms down and he did it right there, on the bare floor. Again and again. I told him, 'I hate you, I'll always hate you now,' and he slapped me. On top of the rape he slapped me and laughed. 'Thanks for letting me hear those old Beatle records,' he said when he left."

"What did you do right afterwards?"

"I was . . . I don't know . . . in a state of shock. And I hurt down there, really hurt. There was blood on my panties. It was so degrading. I ran to the bathroom because I suddenly had to vomit. When I finished vomiting I took a shower and put on a clean nightgown and a robe. I took my bloody panties and my other clothes and went down to the basement and did a load of wash." A rueful grin. "Annemarie thought that was wonderful of me, doing the wash."

"You must have hoped that she'd find out without your telling her."

"I guess I did."

"Does that tell you anything about why you did what you did last Friday night?"

"Oh!" Her face brightened with comprehension. "Yes, I see what you're saying. All this time I've wanted her to . . . even when I agreed to tutor him, I wanted her to catch on . . . guess the truth . . . yes, that's right. And then when she didn't, I . . . just despaired."

"Is that how you felt when your father left for the Coast?"

"In a way. I didn't want Annemarie to know I was upset. I thought that would be disloyal; I mean she'd think I loved him more than her. But at the time I wanted her to suspect . . . to ask me . . . oh God! I've been too good at hiding what I really feel, haven't I? Why would I expect my mother to read my mind? Why?"

Gently, in the remainder of the session, Lucille edged Allison toward an answer to her question.

By the time the hour was over, Lucille felt exhausted. She buzzed Doreen and told her to keep her next patient in the reception room an extra five minutes. Then she closed her eyes, giving herself ten minutes to clear her mind before she called Dave about Colin.

"Must be telepathy," Dave said. "I was just about to call you. Have you had your hour with Allison yet?"

"It's just over, but that's not why I called you. I—"

"Damn! I was hoping . . . Listen, Bannerman just called to tell me that two witnesses saw Allison in her dark green Mustang, driving both east and west on 502 the afternoon of April twentieth. She told me she went right home after school."

"Maybe she forgot," Lucille said, without conviction. Her fear that Allison was directly involved in Billy's murder deepened. "Besides, it's been more than three weeks. Those witnesses must have incredible memories."

"Bannerman said they were reliable. And, you might as well know, she had a motive."

"I *do* know." Lucille paused. "I called you about Colin. He's in Maywood jail."

"Christ, when? Who told you?"

"Simon. He said the MCU men got around him and Conyac's lawyer somehow and he's certain they'll get a confession out of Colin before too long. Dave, we've got to stop them."

"I don't see how—unless you tell me what you know—"

"I can't do that, I simply can't." She realized she sounded hysterical. "I've got another patient waiting."

"Is that your last patient for the day?"

"Yes."

"I'll come by in an hour and we'll see if we can come up with something over a drink."

"But, Dave—" Her intercom buzzed—Doreen to remind her of the waiting patient. "All right. In an hour."

When Dave arrived, she said, "I don't think it's a good idea for us to be seen talking together in late afternoon in a public place. Do you mind staying here?"

Dave looked around her office. "You haven't changed anything. The couch looks a little ragged." He sat in the middle of the couch.

"You think so? I ought to have it recovered." Her fatigue made her sound distracted. And with good reason. Dave was about to confront her with an impossible choice—either to reveal nothing of what she knew about Allison, and so in effect to put the noose around Colin's neck, or to tell Dave everything she knew or suspected and destroy whatever trust Allison had in her, thus destroying all hope of treating Allison successfully.

"Would you like some coffee?" she asked.

"Sure."

Lucille buzzed Doreen and asked her to bring in two coffees, one black, one with a dash of milk, no sugar. Then they waited in uneasy silence until Doreen delivered the coffee and departed.

"First thing, Luce," Dave said, "I realize what your problem is, talking about her to me. But let me fill you in from my side. Remember when we talked about the murder over a week ago? We zeroed in on the gun. Well, the murder weapon still hasn't been found. The MCU boys have gone over the Conyac woods, the farm, the cottages, the main building—inch by inch, with metal detectors, the works, and come up with zilch. We know of only two Magnums in Maywood County. One belonged to Sam Durk and somehow walked out of the State's Attorney's office, and one belongs to a dentist in North Maywood who keeps the gun in a locked gun cabinet. He's the only person with a key to the cabinet. Does anybody else around here own or have access to that kind of gun? We have no way of knowing, because the local farmers don't believe in registering their firearms. So what it comes down to, we've got no smoking gun to identify the murderer because we've got no gun, period.

"Next step," Dave continued. "Find a motive. There we've got ten times more than we need. Billy Durk was one cute kid. His playing around with other guys' girlfriends was the least of it. He got his own best girl, Sally McLeod, to act with him in a dirty movie, then he bragged about it to Sally's friend Allison, your patient, and who knows who else. So right there you have two possibles with a motive—Sally and Allison. Kill Billy and he won't blab anymore, right? But Sally checks out. She didn't leave her grandfather's real-estate office till five-thirty Friday, then went right home and stayed there. We have a tape of her call to the barracks Saturday morning saying she had waited all the previous evening for Billy to show up and take her to a party. So that leaves your patient. She had motive and she's been placed in the vicinity of the crime by two witnesses. Her stepfather has a gun, but it's not a Magnum. So we go back to my theory that Billy got hold of the gun from the S.A.'s office and had it with him when the murderer confronted him."

"Was there evidence of a struggle? Or could he have been shot by accident?"

"Well, no. The shot was fired from some distance away, struck the back of his head and lodged in the occipital ridge."

"So the murder weapon is still a problem."

"I don't think so. And I'll tell you why." Dave finished his coffee and set the empty cup on a corner of Lucille's desk. "Let's say Allison saw Billy's new bike outside the McLeod real-estate office. When Billy left the office to see his brother, Allison followed him. Then when Billy turned into the old logging road, she drove in after him. Billy thought he was irrestible to all women, so he probably figured she followed him because she wanted to admire his new toy. He says to her, 'Look what else I got!' and shows her the Magnum he's taken from the S.A.'s office. She asks if she can hold it and he says sure, why not? He's full of himself, he's a real big shot. That's in character. So she heads back to her car, and when she's about thirty feet away, she turns around, takes dead aim, and fires."

"And what does she do with the gun?" Lucille asked.

"She takes it with her. And probably throws it out the car window when she's driving home."

"Then you'll be looking for the gun on both sides of 502?"

"I've already called Bannerman. Of course, I've also got to get a warrant to search Grunewald's house and farm, just in case she hid it there."

Lucille reviewed Dave's script. She saw a number of

holes in it, beginning with Dave's reconstruction of the relationship between Billy and Allison. "I don't see Billy
handing Allison a gun and then turning his back on her
while she walks away with it," she said. "You're dead wrong
about the way Allison felt toward Billy. She hated him and
he knew it. He would have had to be incredibly stupid to
put a gun in her hands, and we know Billy wasn't stupid."

"Not stupid, no," Dave said, "but maybe overconfi-
dent where women were concerned. He thought no woman
could resist him. If she said she hated him, he'd figure it
was only an act."

Lucille shook her head. "Billy *knew* Allison hated him,
and he knew why."

"Because of the dirty movie?"

"No. More than that."

"You won't tell me?"

"I can't."

"But you're sure of it?"

"Absolutely."

"So—" Dave hunched his shoulders—another gesture
borrowed from whom—Kojak? "I'll have to figure out some
other way to put a gun in her hands. And I've got some
other possibles. Tell me what you think of them." Dryly he
told her about Billy's attempted extortion of Ellis Somers
and Dane Farnol. He also described his meeting with Garrison Craig.

"But Somers's alibi checks out," Lucille said.

"Yes. All the way."

"And the money Billy was asking wasn't worth Farnol
paying to have Billy killed."

"That's the way I see it. Anyway, it doesn't look like a
contract killing. A hired gun could have hit Billy while he
was riding his bike on 502. A contractor wouldn't risk going
into some narrow little road in the woods he didn't know

where it led to. In fact, the one thing I'm sure of about the murder is that the murderer is somebody local, somebody who knows the county, somebody who's lived here awhile."

Lucille lunged at the straw. "Allison wouldn't have known about the logging road."

"She might have. If she ever visited Colin. That's a question I'll have to ask her."

"What are you going to do about Colin?"

"Nothing I *can* do." His narrowed eyes accused her. "Unless you tell me why Billy would be sure Allison hated him."

Lucille rubbed her cheek, remembering that Billy had slapped Allison after he'd raped her. "If you find the gun where you say it is, I'll tell you."

"Okay, Doctor." Dave smiled. "If I promise not to bug you about Allison, will you have dinner with me Saturday night?"

"I'd love to." She returned the smile, then frowned. "Dave, please, don't be rough on her. Even if she *is* guilty—"

Dave had his hand on the door. He wheeled around, scowling. "So you agree with me, do you?"

"I didn't say that."

"I'd like to know what the hell you're not telling me."

"Dave, you bring back bad memories when you act like this." She took her handbag out of a desk drawer. "I'm going home." As she neared the door, he grabbed her shoulders and held her facing him. "All right, Dr. Superior. You just sit on what you know and let Colin fry. Because that's what he's going to do."

With effort she kept her voice calm. "I said I'd tell you if you found the gun."

"And if we don't?"

"I can't say. It depends on—" Dave dug his fingers into her shoulders. "Please let me go."

He released his hold. "You're a bitch, a gold-plated bitch. What do you think you're doing? Practicing triage? Your classy patient, with the fashion-model face and good grades, is worth more than poor dumb Colin, who probably figures by now it's his job in life to take the rap for everybody. Isn't that it?"

"No, Dave. I would never keep silent if telling what I knew would save Colin."

"And what if you're too late?" Dave swung the door open roughly. "Forget about Saturday night. I don't think my appetite will be too good by then."

The story made the Sunday edition of *The New York Times.* The report, in the lower left-hand corner of the front page, was headed MAYWOOD YOUTH CONFESSES. The story began:

> Under interrogation by police, Colin Durk, 15, confessed yesterday that he had killed his brother William Durk, 18, on April 20. The brother's body was found April 27 in a wooded area a short distance from the Connecticut Youth Academy farm where Colin Durk was working as a farmhand.
>
> The younger Durk was sentenced to a year at the Youth Academy, Connecticut's model facility for juvenile offenders, on September 28, 1983, after confessing that he had killed his father, Samuel Durk, with a shotgun on August 10, 1983. The killing was witnessed by the youth's brother and his mother, Mae Durk. Both witnesses testified in court that Colin had picked up the gun to stop his father from beating his mother. William testified that he had tried to wrest

the gun from his brother and the gun may have fired accidentally.

The lenient sentence given Colin Durk for the murder of his father is unlikely to be repeated for the alleged murder of his brother. According to the State's Attorney's office, the 15-year-old youth will be tried in Criminal Court as an adult. . . .

The story wasn't news to Dave. Santini had called him Saturday afternoon, after Dave had returned from taking his exam in Intermediate Russian. "It's not a phony," Santini said. "You got any doubts, come on by this afternoon and listen to the tape."

"I'll be right there."

The confession was not quite as airtight as Santini insisted it was. Dave played the crucial section three times.

SANTINI: What made you go into the woods?

DURK: I was in the upper field and I saw Billy on 502.

SANTINI: Had your brother met you in the woods on other occasions?

DURK: Yes, sir.

SANTINI: So when you saw him riding his motorcycle on Route 502, you assumed he was on his way to see you?

DURK: Yes, sir.

SANTINI: How long would you say it was between the time you saw Billy on the highway and you met him in the woods?

DURK: I don't know. Five or ten minutes maybe. I had to finish what I was doing.

SANTINI: What happened when you met your brother in the woods?

DURK: I can't remember. I just saw him.

SANTINI: What did he say to you?

DURK: I don't remember.

SANTINI: But you remember seeing him, don't you?

DURK: I remember seeing him lying on the ground, looking at the sky.

SANTINI: But before that, what happened?

DURK: I don't remember.

SANTINI: Do you remember a struggle?

DURK: I guess there must have been a struggle.

SANTINI: About what?

DURK: Well, about the gun. That's what you—

SANTINI: What did you do with the gun?

DURK: I must have fired it. Like you—

SANTINI: How many times did you fire the gun?

DURK: I don't know. Once, I guess.

SANTINI: Where were you standing when you fired the gun?

DURK: I don't remember.

SANTINI: What did you do with the gun after you fired it?

DURK: Threw it away, I guess.

SANTINI: Where did you throw the gun?

DURK: In the woods where you—

SANTINI: So the gun you fired is somewhere in the woods, is that right?

DURK: I guess so.

It seemed obvious to Dave that prior to the taping, Santini and his colleagues had fed Colin their version of Billy's murder, and Colin had bought it. He'd assumed their version must be correct, even where it contradicted his own experience. Whenever, on the tape, Colin tried to indicate he'd been coached, Santini cut him off.

A skillful attorney could make hash of Colin's confession. Unfortunately, there was almost no chance Colin would get a skillful attorney to defend him. If Dave failed to find who actually killed Billy Durk, Colin would, at the very least, spend the next twenty years of his young life in prison.

After listening to the tape, Dave confronted Santini. "Your so-called confession smells. I'm going to have to talk to Colin myself. How soon can I see him?"

"Not till Monday. But you'll be wasting your time."

Santini sounded annoyingly self-confident. Dave glared at him. "Let's get this straight, Santini. Our job is to protect the citizens, right? Do you see where throwing a fifteen-year-old boy in prison for the rest of his life for a crime he probably didn't commit is protecting the citizens? Tell me if I'm wrong." He stood over Santini, who seemed to shrink back into his swivel chair.

"Listen, I'm not out to railroad the kid, but have you got anything else?" Santini's voice was plaintive. "The citizens are asking us to solve this crime."

"We'll solve it. But not like this." Dave started for the door. "By the way, when am I going to see that videotape I asked you to get?"

"We had to work through a judge in L.A. I think he ordered the Amphitryon outfit to release it yesterday or the day before. It should be here Monday or Tuesday at the latest. . . . You're welcome," Santini added.

"Yeah, thanks. I'll be over at the county jail Monday morning. Don't worry about taping it. I'll bring my own machine." Dave slammed the door.

The newspaper story only deepened his anger. He was angry with himself, he was angry with Santini, he was angry with Lucille. On top of all that, he was positive he'd flunked the Russian exam. His dream of leaving the boondocks for a big-time administrative job was blurring. Sometimes, recently, he'd begun to question whether that was what he really wanted. Eventually he'd make captain in the State Police. Would that be so bad?

The question had come up the first time he'd met Lucille's mother. He and Lucille went to her studio near Lincoln Center. Estelle Esker was an imposing woman. Her worldwide reputation as an opera coach was based on an unerring ear, impeccable taste, and thoroughgoing musicality. Her students, among whom were numbered some of the world's most famous opera stars, were terrified of her. She advised them not only about their singing but about their romances, their financial affairs, their houses, their children—her curiosity was unrestrained and her opinions, however arbitrary, were delivered with Jehovah-like finality.

Lucille introduced Dave as "Lieutenant David Littlejohn."

Mrs. Esker barely looked at him. She eyed her daughter accusingly. "So you've got yourself a soldier. You'll have to travel a lot and he could get killed. Would you like that?"

"He's not a soldier. He's a policeman, a state trooper," Lucille said.

"That's worse. The police are fascists. You don't know what you're doing." Lucille's mother proceeded to narrate a half dozen cautionary tales of young women who had suffered unspeakable abuse as a result of marrying fascists. Throughout her narration she spoke as if Dave weren't there.

When her monologue finally wound down, she at last faced Dave and gave him a wide smile. "Well, maybe a state trooper could be a good career. You'll be a big shot—a general, a captain maybe? You love her? You'll take care of her? Go, get married—with my blessing."

Why hadn't their marriage worked? Why had they dug their opposing trenches so deep?

What's past is past, he told himself. Why couldn't he leave it alone?

Early Monday, before Dave left for the barracks, Bannerman phoned to report that a third witness had come forward who had seen Allison on Route 502 that Friday afternoon. But a search on either side of the highway, from the logging road west and south to the Grunewald farm, had failed to locate a gun.

Dave had obtained the search warrant on Friday, but he held off searching the Grunewald house and farm until he could be certain Allison wouldn't be there. He took Harry with him, and shortly after 9 A.M. they stood at the farmhouse door. Dave showed Annemarie the search warrant.

"I don't understand," she said. "Billy hasn't been here in ages, not since before spring vacation."

Dave didn't say it was her daughter he suspected. He merely said, "We have a lead we have to follow up. We'll try not to mess things up too much."

While Dave searched Allison's room and the rest of the house, Harry searched the barn and sheds and looked for signs of dug soil in the yard around the house. All the fields had been plowed and seeded recently, so it would take a large crew armed with metal detectors to look for the gun there.

The searches were fruitless. Before leaving, Dave said to Annemarie: "Please have Allison phone me at the barracks as soon as she gets home from school."

"You sure about this?" Harry said in the car. "Enough to call in an army to go over the fields? It's bigger than the

Conyac farm and you'd sure raise hell with Marty's spring sowing."

"Goddamn, I don't know," Dave said.

At the barracks, Dave put the official tape recorder in his car and took off for the Maywood jail.

The county prison was by no means a modern facility for incarceration. Built of granite from a nearby quarry at the turn of the century, it housed thirty-five prisoners at full capacity. It hadn't been filled to capacity since the 1960s when the police had erroneously tried to teach a lesson to some rowdy demonstrators and had been sued for unlawful arrest. The police had won the case, but the legal fees for their defense had aroused Maywood County taxpayers.

The cells on the upper three stories were small and dark. The stone building was always cold and damp, even in midsummer.

Dave met Colin in one of the small offices on the ground floor. Colin sat impassively while Dave tested the recording equipment. A prison guard stood in a corner, his hand on his gun belt.

"You miss being out on the farm, a day like this?" Dave began. Colin nodded.

"The recorder can't hear it if you nod or shake your head."

"Yeah. Yes, sir."

"When you told Sergeant Santini how you saw your brother's dead body, did you think that would get the police off your back, make them stop questioning you, let you go back to Conyac?"

"Sort of."

"Did they promise you you could go back to Conyac and work on the farm?"

"They said I might." Colin paused. "If I told them—"

"Told them what?"

"How Billy died."

"Do you know for sure how your brother died?"

"Honest, sir, I don't remember. I must have blacked out."

"Is that what the sergeant said happened?"

"Yes, sir."

"But you do remember seeing Billy's dead body?"

"Yes, sir."

"I questioned you twice—once on the phone when Billy was reported missing and once in person right after we found his body. Do you remember those interrogations?"

"Yes, sir."

"If you saw your brother's dead body on Friday, April twentieth, then when I asked you on the phone on Monday, April twenty-third, if you knew where your brother was and you said no, you weren't telling me the truth, were you?"

"No, sir."

"And after we found Billy's body on Friday, April twenty-seventh, and I questioned you in Dr. Dennis's office, you didn't tell me the truth then either, did you?"

"No, sir."

"Why didn't you want me to know you'd seen your brother dead?"

"I didn't know how it happened."

"You told the detectives that you shot him."

"That's what they said must have happened. I just didn't remember."

"Do you remember hearing a gunshot?"

"No, sir."

"Do you remember hearing anybody moving around—leaves crackling or branches breaking?"

"No, sir. It was wet."

"Did you see anybody?"

"No, sir."

"What about when you got out of the woods and looked over at the highway? Did you see anybody then?"

"No. No, sir." Fear tightened Colin's thin face.

"Maybe you saw a car driving away, a car you recognized."

"I didn't look over at the highway after—after I saw Billy."

"Did you see a gun near Billy's body?"

"No, sir."

"Did you touch the body?"

"No. I could see he was dead."

"Please describe how he was lying when you saw him on Friday, April twentieth."

"He was all sprawled out on top of the leaves."

"Was he lying face down in the mud and leaves? Is that how you knew he was dead?"

"He was looking at the sky. His eyes were kind of staring."

"Why didn't you tell anybody at Conyac you'd found your brother's body? You knew we were looking for him."

"I was scared."

"Scared of what?"

"Just scared."

"Scared that the person who killed Billy might kill you?"

Colin's lips quivered. "Oh no, sir."

"Might kill you because you knew who she was?" Dave had chosen the pronoun deliberately.

"How did you—?" Colin clapped his hand over his mouth, a swift involuntary gesture.

Dave bent over the boy. "Colin, I promise you, tell me who killed your brother and I won't tell anyone—not a soul—where I got the information. You'll be one hundred percent safe. That's a promise. Don't you want the person who killed Billy to pay for it? Don't you realize that the MCU detectives can use your confession to put you in jail for the rest of your life? And the real murderer will go free. That's not fair, is it? Not fair to Billy or to you."

Colin sat like a stone. His eyes were half closed. He gave no sign that he'd heard a word.

"Think about it. Think about throwing away your whole life for no good reason. Think about your mother. She'll be all alone, Billy and your dad dead and you in jail for ever and ever. And here she was, counting on you being out of Conyac in a few months so you could help her take care of the house and maybe put in a few crops next spring on the acres you got left that your dad didn't sell to the developers."

At the word "crops," Colin's eyes opened slightly, but otherwise he remained motionless.

"Let's go over this once more. You don't have to say anything, so it won't go on the tape. Just nod for yes or shake your head for no. Okay?" The boy gave no indication he would follow Dave's instructions. "Now, did you see the person who shot Billy?"

Colin shook his head.

"Did you see a car on 502 that you recognized?"

Again he shook his head.

"Did a man kill Billy?"

A slight pause, then a head shake.

"Did a girl or woman kill Billy?"

Another pause, another head shake.

Some of Colin's denials had to be false. To continue was useless.

"I want you to think about what I said—about your mother, especially. And I'll keep hoping you wake up to what's going to happen to you if they nail you for your brother's murder. I just hope you wake up before it's too late." Dave told the guard waiting in the corner to escort Colin back to his cell.

Back at the barracks he found a message to call Dr. Esker.

"I think I've found a way out of our—our impasse," Lucille said. "When are you planning to question Allison?"

"Probably late this afternoon, when she gets home from school."

"Have you found the gun?"

"I can't answer you, Luce."

"That means you haven't." A pause. "Well, here's my idea. If I'm there when you interrogate her, she'll know firsthand that I haven't violated confidentiality. At the same time I provide you with a witness that your questioning didn't invade her rights."

"You could also encourage her to withhold information," Dave said.

"If she's a suspect, she has a right to have a lawyer present during an interrogation. Would you rather have me or a lawyer?"

"She could still ask for a lawyer. And a judge could throw out your testimony on the grounds of suspected collusion. We used to be married, remember."

"Even so, I should be there when you question her. She's a patient and I have a right to be concerned about her."

"Tell you what. I'll interrogate her in your office. It's a friendly environment, wouldn't you say? But you've got to promise me you won't try to squelch her if she's about to reveal incriminating information."

"I promise. What time should I expect you? I'm free after four."

"I'll bring Allison to your office at four-thirty."

Early in the afternoon Dave received a call from Sandra Murphy.

"You'll never believe this," Sandra said. "When I went into the property room this morning, the missing Durk gun, the Magnum you were looking for, it was right there on the shelf. You couldn't miss it."

"Any fingerprints?"

"Not a chance. The gun looked like patent leather, it had so much polish on it. I sent it over to Ballistics to see if it matches the bullet they took out of Billy's head."

"When will you know?"

"Tomorrow sometime. I'll call you."

"Thanks."

Could Allison somehow have entered the S.A.'s property room over the weekend and put the gun back? She knew she'd become a suspect. She had to get rid of the gun before the police searched her room.

Dave called Bannerman. "Find out if anyone saw that same dark green Mustang anywhere near the State's Attorney's office anytime between last Friday evening and Sunday night."

"Will do," Bannerman said.

Dave next called Santini. The videotape hadn't yet arrived from the Coast. "I'll call you as soon as it comes in," Santini said.

Dave found it difficult to concentrate on routine. His muscles itched for action. Staying seated behind a desk was painful.

Was Allison the murderer? She had motive and she

was smart. By changing her pattern of behavior prior to murdering Billy, she'd got her mother to put her in the care of a psychotherapist—a neat foundation for an insanity defense.

Allison called him at 3:45, and he told her he'd come around and pick her up. "I'd like to interrogate you in Dr. Esker's presence, so we'll go to her office, if that's all right with you," he said.

"That's not usual, is it?"

"No. But it's legal."

She was waiting for him in the road in front of the house. He noticed Annemarie looking out a window, watching her. "Are you going to arrest me?" Allison said, with an oddly satisfied smile.

"Why?" Dave said, as they drove off. "Do you think you should be arrested?"

"Of course not. I haven't done anything."

"I hope so." His tone was icy. He wasn't impervious to the girl's beauty.

"Are you going to put me in handcuffs?"

"Are you planning to run away?"

"No."

Inside Lucille's office, with Lucille as witness, he read Allison her rights.

"Why didn't you tell me I was a suspect and needed a lawyer before I got into your car?" Allison asked, with the same odd smile.

"I didn't interrogate you in the car," Dave said. The girl's flippancy set him wondering. Maybe she really was crazy. "Do you want to call a lawyer?"

Lucille sat on the couch. Allison sat next to her and took her hand. "I trust Dr. Esker," Allison said. "She's better than a lawyer."

"Thank you," Lucille said.

Dave started the tape recorder, establishing the time and place of the interrogation and the identity of the participants. He turned to Allison. "A week ago, Monday, May seventh, when I questioned you at your home, you told me that on Friday, April twentieth, you came straight home from Maywood High and remained at home, without going out, for the rest of the day. Is that correct?"

"Yes."

"But we now have three witnesses who say they saw you, in your dark green Mustang, traveling both east and west on Route 502 on that same Friday afternoon. How do you explain that?"

"I must have forgotten about going out."

"What were you doing on Route 502?"

"Going shopping, I suppose."

"What did you buy?"

"I don't remember. Oh, some pantyhose."

"At what store did you buy the hose?"

"It must have been Brandel's."

"Did you pay cash or use a credit card?"

Allison gave Dave a sidelong, appraising look. "I paid cash."

"Do you have a receipt for your purchase?"

"Of course not."

"While you were in your car, did you notice Billy Durk on his new motorcycle riding on Route 502?"

"No."

"Did you see Billy Durk on Friday afternoon, April twentieth?"

"No."

"While you were shopping, did you meet any friends?"

"No."

"Might the clerk at Brandel's remember you?"

"I doubt it."

"Did you buy anything else?"

"I don't think so."

"You're not sure?"

She shook her head. Lucille squeezed her hand.

"Let's go back a ways. Have you ever visited Colin while he's been at Conyac?"

"Yes. I feel sorry for him."

"When you want to visit Colin, what part of Conyac do you go to?"

"The main building, of course. Then they call his cottage and he comes over."

"Did you ever visit him while he was working on the Conyac farm?"

She paused. "I don't remember."

"If you wanted to see Colin while he was outside working, how would you do it?"

"I don't know what you mean."

"How would you get to the farm? Would you go to the main building first?"

"Probably. A visitor has to get permission."

"Conyac doesn't give visitors permission to talk to the boys while they're working, do they?"

"I don't know." She sounded sullen.

"When you visited Colin on the farm, how did you reach the farm?"

Allison withdrew her hand from under Lucille's. "I didn't say I visited Colin on the farm."

"You said you didn't remember." Dave smiled. "Would you like me to run the tape back?"

She shook her head. She looked irritated rather than frightened.

"Then let's assume," Dave continued, "that you

wanted to speak to Colin while he was out at the farm. How would you get there?"

"Walk across the fields, I guess."

"All the way up from the farm manager's house? Don't you know there's a shorter way, a shortcut?"

"Is there?" She turned to Lucille. "This is ridiculous. Why is he asking me such silly questions?"

"He has his reasons," Lucille said.

"You don't know of any shortcut to the farm, say from off 502?" Dave persisted.

"Obviously not."

"What if I told you we have a witness who saw you turn your car into the old logging road that runs between Route 502 and the farm?"

Did she catch her breath? He couldn't be sure.

"The witness would be lying," she said with eerie poise. "I don't know anything about old logging roads."

"And you don't know anything about guns either. Is that right?"

"I told you. I hate guns."

"I understand that when you came to live here your stepfather, Marty Grunewald, taught your mother and you how to fire a pistol. Constable Sam Burns discussed with your stepfather how to set up a target range a safe distance from the road, and later the constable observed you and your mother target-shooting. Do you remember that?"

"That was stupid. I only hit the bull's-eye once."

"Sam Burns said you and your mother learned how to handle a gun pretty well. Do you want to revise your statement about guns?"

"No. I hate them. If Sam Durk hadn't kept so many guns around, he'd be alive today." Her voice was edged with contempt.

"Possibly." The interrogation wasn't going well. Dave

felt constrained by Lucille's presence. The muted colors of her office seemed to discourage confrontation. Yet he knew Allison was skirting the truth when she wasn't lying outright.

"Allison," Lucille said quietly, "wouldn't you feel better if you told the lieutenant the truth about that afternoon?"

Dave looked at her, surprised. He hadn't expected her to help.

"What afternoon?" Allison said.

"You know what afternoon." Lucille's voice was gently admonishing.

"I told you. I went shopping."

"Then why are you frightened?"

The question hung in the air for several seconds. "I'm not frightened," Allison said finally, but her voice shook.

Dave interpreted Lucille's intervention as a go-ahead.

"I shouldn't have to remind you," he said, "that withholding evidence is a crime." He eyed her so coldly, she turned her head as if to ward off a blow. "If you saw anything on Route 502 that Friday afternoon that would help us solve Billy's murder, you're required to tell me what you saw."

"I didn't see anything." She tossed her head. "Frankly, you're wasting your time."

In Dave's experience, when anyone said "frankly," what followed was almost always a lie. "I think you saw Billy. I think you saw him turn into the old logging road. I think you turned into that same road after him."

"That's not so!" She turned to Lucille. "Why are you just sitting there? He's trying to pin Billy's murder on me. And he's wrong. All wrong! I didn't do it! I never even got near Billy."

"Are you saying then that you saw him in the distance?" Lucille asked.

"No. I didn't say that."

"I thought you did." Lucille smiled at Dave.

"You did," he said. "You said you didn't get near him, which implies that you saw him far away."

Allison seemed to crumple. "Oh well, what if I did see him riding that ridiculous machine. I didn't give it a second thought."

The girl's sudden shifts from fear to flippancy were unnerving. Dave knew enough about psychology to recognize Allison's unpredictable responses to his questions as a symptom of her troubled emotional state. "Please describe exactly where and when it was you saw Billy," he said. "Was it while you were going east on 502 toward Brandel's or coming back?"

"Going east. I didn't really go to Brandel's." Her voice was low, almost inaudible. She held Lucille's hand tightly.

"You didn't buy anything at Brandel's then? You didn't buy pantyhose or anything else?"

"No."

"But instead of going home after school, you drove your car in the opposite direction. Why did you do that?"

"To see Colin. I thought someone should tell him what Billy was saying—that he'd kill him when he got out of Conyac. I thought someone should warn him."

"Did you see Colin on Friday, April twentieth?"

"No."

"Why not?"

"I saw Billy up ahead of me, on the motorcycle. He slowed down all of a sudden and turned in the logging road."

"Did you turn in the road after him?"

"No. I didn't follow him. Why would I? I didn't want

154

to be anywhere near him." She paused. Her breath came in short gasps. "Do you always have to solve a crime? Billy deserved to die. He was evil. Whoever killed him did the right thing." Her pale green eyes appealed to him for agreement.

Dave ignored her appeal, despite Lucille's worried look. "After you saw him turn into the road, what did you do?"

"I turned around in Brandel's parking lot and came home."

"And that's all you did? You didn't see anything suspicious? You didn't see anyone following Billy?"

"I did not see any person following Billy."

Dave wondered at the precision of her answer. And what had happened to the fear she'd revealed earlier in the questioning? It appeared that she'd discovered a way of satisfying her need to tell the truth without endangering herself.

"I must ask you once more—did you see anyone or anything that might help us to identify Billy's murderer?"

"I saw no one." The odd smile returned.

"Do you know of anyone who would be happy to see Billy dead?"

"Me." She lifted her chin. "But I didn't kill him."

"Anybody else?"

"Ellis Somers. He lives across the road."

"How do you know about that?"

"Billy told me. He always had to brag about how smart he was, but Mr. Somers never gave him any money."

"I gather from what you said at our earlier meeting that Billy also told you about the sexually explicit videotape he made with Sally in Florida."

"How did you find out?" Her voice rose. "Who told you?"

"Garrison Craig." The answer appeared to calm her. "Do you know if Billy was planning to use the video in another extortion scheme? Like the one he tried on Somers?"

"He didn't say. I saw him only once after spring vacation. But it's possible. I mean, it's a motive for murder, isn't it?"

"Yes." Dave smiled in encouragement. "Who might he have gone to?"

She remained silent for several seconds. Finally she said, "Sally, of course."

"Would she be able to get four thousand dollars?"

"Not easily."

"Couldn't Sally have asked her grandfather for the money?"

"No! Never! He'd know she wanted it for Billy."

"We'll have to look further then, won't we, if we're going to find the real murderer and keep Colin out of jail for the rest of his life." Dave turned off the recorder on Lucille's desk. "Let's get you home."

"I'll drive Allison home," Lucille said.

"Okay with you?" Dave asked Allison.

Allison nodded. Dave saw her eyes flash angrily at him as he left.

Allison looked pale and tense. Lucille put her arm around the girl's shoulders. "Was that as bad as you thought it might be?" she asked.

"He was just doing his job." Allison shrugged off Lucille's comforting arm. "I can see why you divorced him."

"Can you?" Lucille rose from the couch.

"Does he really think I killed Billy?"

"I think he strongly suspected you at the beginning of the interrogation, but now he's not so sure."

"I didn't do it. Do *you* believe me?"

"Yes, I believe you."

"I could have done it, though. And then if they executed me, I wouldn't have anything more to worry about."

"It's not uncommon for people who want to kill themselves to kill someone else."

"I know that." Allison sounded impatient. "But I didn't do it."

On the ride home, Allison made no further protestations of innocence. She had the relaxed air of someone who has unexpectedly triumphed over an implacable foe. How little Allison knew about Dave's methods! Although he had only briefly shown the harshness he was capable of, he had in fact elicited from Allison the information he sought. The questions Allison had answered with a lie or a diversion told him as much as the truthful answers.

In the evening Lucille phoned him. "I want to thank you for the way you conducted the interrogation. I don't think it upset Allison too much."

"I didn't dig out the real reason she hated Billy, did I? Are you still maintaining that's privileged?"

"Yes, Dave. And you don't need it to solve the crime. If ever Allison comes to trial, it might come out as part of her defense. Not before."

"I guess I'll have to take your word for that." He hung up abruptly.

Damn him. Why had she bothered to thank him?

He surprised her with a call at eleven the following morning. "I thought I should let you know," he said. "Your patient is out. At least for now."

"Why? What happened?"

"The Durk gun, the Magnum that I thought might be the murder weapon, reappeared in the S.A.'s property room over the weekend. Ballistics checked if it was the gun that fired the bullet they took out of Billy's skull. It's not."

"Are they sure?"

"As sure as Ballistics ever gets. So there goes my theory. Bannerman's crew have scoured both sides of 502, and my troopers have looked along Highfields Road and West Road. Nothing. The MCU is giving the Conyac farm a third going-over. They're certain the gun is there."

"That means they're going to indict Colin, doesn't it?"

"No way to stop them unless Allison speaks up."

"That's not fair, Dave. I won't let you unload your frustration on me."

"Tell that to Colin."

CHAPTER

8

At MCU headquarters a good-sized crowd had gathered in the screening room for the premiere showing of *A Guide to Intimate Relationships,* the title Craig had given the video. Almost the entire MCU detective force, male and female, was there, along with those civilian employees who felt they couldn't afford to pass up a memorable experience.

The movie began with Garrison Craig's voice—a cross between John Cameron Swayze and Dan Rather— explaining that it was an educational video for use primarily by sex therapists. Besides a crudely lettered credit naming Craig as the director and Columbus Educational Enterprises as the producer, there were no other credits. The actors' names were not given.

Almost from the first it was apparent that *A Guide to Intimate Relationships* was, as Santini said later, "the funniest movie I've seen since *Horse Feathers.*" The contrast between Craig's orotund syllables, suitable for a Public Broadcasting documentary on the Nile, and the wooden movements of the three actors, fumbling to take off each other's clothes, then lying atop or beneath one another like an animated ham sandwich, was the stuff of which great slapstick comedy is made. The actors had no speaking lines. Craig's narration had obviously been added after Farnol had seen the tape in Florida.

The video lasted fifteen minutes. At its conclusion there was a round of applause. As they left the screening room, the viewers were wiping away tears of laughter.

In his office Santini asked Dave, "The video tell you anything you didn't know?"

Dave shook his head. "As pornography it's pretty tame. I had an idea Billy might have tried to blackmail his girlfriend, but there's not a clear shot of Sally McLeod anywhere. Maybe Craig cut it out."

"But would the McLeod girl have known she wasn't identifiable?"

"Probably not. There's no question she was terrified when I questioned her."

"You told me her alibi checked out."

"It did. But not necessarily for later that day. She could have left her grandparents' house in the early evening without their knowing she was gone."

"Then where was Billy all that time? He was seen on 502 around three-thirty in the afternoon. Colin saw him on the road around the same time, and in the woods about ten minutes later. You can't quarrel with that part of Colin's confession. We've got witnesses."

"Maybe Sally had someone cover for her in the real-estate office and followed Billy when he left."

"You're reaching, Lieutenant. . She has a silver-gray Toyota. It never left the parking space behind the real-estate office until after five."

"There's no way I can get you to hold off charging Colin?"

"Not unless you come up with something by Tuesday at the latest."

With difficulty Dave repressed an overwhelming urge to wipe the supercilious grin off Santini's face. "You'll hear from me," he said, sounding far more confident than he felt.

The Wednesday session with Allison was a disaster. When Lucille told her that she was pretty sure Dave no longer considered her a prime suspect, Allison's response was hostile.

"I don't like you talking about me behind my back. It isn't ethical. It isn't professional. Besides, Colin confessed, and that's that. We're supposed to talk about me here, not anyone else."

"You don't live alone in the world," Lucille said. "You relate to and are affected by other people."

"My gracious, what an original insight!" Her sarcasm was unleavened by a smile. "Your capacity for deep philosophic thought astounds me."

Allison maintained her disagreeable tone throughout the session. The wall she had erected around herself was higher than ever. The only way for Lucille to get on with the job of helping Allison dismantle the wall was to put Billy's murder aside.

She told Dave of her decision over Sunday brunch at a new Maywood restaurant furnished with pale woods and white Formica-topped tables. Outside, the sun was high in a cloudless sky. The occasional breeze still carried a bite, but otherwise it was a perfect day for golf. Dave must have wanted to see her badly to forgo his Sunday golf game.

"You may be finished with Billy's murder, but I'm not," Dave said grimly. "All I need is one break. Maywood and Highfields are too small to keep something like this secret. I'd lay even money there are at least a half dozen people who know right now who the murderer is, the real murderer. And eventually one of them will talk. You can count on it."

"Before Colin comes to trial?"

"With any luck. Otherwise we see to it he gets a good lawyer, if I have to pay for it myself."

"I'll help," she said. She looked up at the young waitress who had arrived with their omelets and sausages. "Is Colin still in the Maywood jail?" she asked Dave.

"No. The S.A. figured they'd look better in court if they sent him back to Conyac. They put him in Cottage Eleven—the one with bars on the windows. If he comes out of that place okay, it'll be some kind of miracle."

"Any idea who took the Durk gun away and then put it back?"

Dave grinned. "No. And I guarantee that's one mystery that won't be solved. Want to know why?"

He was teasing her. When they were married he liked to make fun of her attempts to play detective. The patronizing air he adopted when guarding his professional turf annoyed her. "No, I don't particularly want to know why," she said.

"Good." The grin vanished. He speared a slice of avocado, used as a garnish, and regarded it thoughtfully. "Would you say that Allison knows who the murderer is?"

"Yes, I'd say she does. From her pattern of responses during the interrogation—anxiety when it appeared you were getting close, relief when you were barking up the wrong tree—yes, she must know."

"I've played the tape over. You can hear her voice get tight. If we rule her out as the guilty party, then we have to conclude that she knows who the guilty party is. Just from the sound of her voice."

"When did you think her voice sounded the most anxious?"

"Two times. First when I asked her if she saw anything on 502 that would help us solve the murder. She denied she saw anything, but her voice is a dead giveaway. Second time when I asked if she saw anyone following Billy. Her answer was very strange, and again her voice was constricted."

Lucille nodded.

Dave gave her a sly look. "So what do we do now?" He was sparring with her again.

"I see where you're heading. You want me to say, 'Go ahead, give Allison the third degree. It's all right with me.' Well, I'm not going to say that. She was in terrible shape on Wednesday. I thought she'd handled the interrogation pretty well, but I was wrong. It just about wiped out any progress we'd made since I started seeing her. So, no, you can't grill her again. Absolutely not." She knew now why he'd passed up a round of golf in order to see her. She looked down at her plate. "This restaurant isn't going to make it. My omelet is overdone."

"You let it get cold." Dave poured each of them more of the house white wine. "The investigation of Billy's murder is getting cold, too. Do you honestly want to see his murderer get away with it? Honestly?"

"You'll get a break."

"Not without helping it along."

"You'll have to help it along in another direction. I can't permit you to subject Allison to further interrogation."

"The S.A.'s office could bring her in as a material witness."

"Based on what? The sound of her voice on your

163

tape?" She flung her napkin over the cold omelet. "Get the check, please."

All in all, it was not a pleasant brunch.

The break Dave hoped for came the following day, although he didn't recognize it at the time.

It was late Monday afternoon. Sergeant Hillis, who was about to go off duty, was in Dave's office giving a hole-by-hole account of his Sunday golf game, which he'd shot in a two-over-par 74. He'd come to the seventeenth hole when he paused at the sound of an immediately identifiable voice in the outer office.

"I demand to see Lieutenant Littlejohn without further delay," said Garrison Craig.

"He's busy," Phil said. "He has someone in his office."

Dave opened the door and Hillis departed, leaving untold the chronicle of his brilliant shots on the seventeenth and eighteenth holes of the Maywood Golf Club.

"C'mon in."

Craig, his face blotched with outrage, entered Dave's office. "I'd like to know who gave you authority to show *Guide to Intimate Relationships*. That tape is my property. Showing it in its rough, unedited version has damaged me professionally. Its potential commercial value has been severely diminished. I plan to sue you and Maywood County for unlawful expropriation of private property. And that's only number one."

"Hold on. Have a seat."

Craig squeezed himself into the chair. "You'll be served with papers within the week. I've got a lawyer working on it right now."

"Then your lawyer must already have discovered that we had a court order to the Amphitryon company to release the tape because of its possible bearing on the murder of

William Durk. We did nothing illegal or actionable." He regarded Craig with mild amusement. "You said that was number one. What's number two?"

Craig continued snorting fire. "You won't get away with it. Here's one citizen who won't be squashed by the mighty power of bureaucracy. You'll have to answer for the damage you've done me."

"Is that your second problem?"

Craig thrust out his heavy jaw. His jowls quivered. "No. And don't think you can make light of it. I'm within my rights to seek compensation for damages. If it has to come out of your pocket, that's too bad. I came forward of my own volition and without expectation of reward. Instead of gratitude you humiliate me. But you won't get away with it." Craig rested his crossed arms on his ample belly.

"I'm sorry," Dave said, "that there wasn't a more favorable response to your video, but cops aren't your ideal audience. I'm sure when you show the final version of the video to sex therapists, they'll be much more appreciative."

"There's not going to be a final version. You've destroyed any chance for me to get additional funding. Worse, you're directly responsible for my being evicted from my home of many years. I demand redress."

"You mean Sundergaard has asked you to leave?"

"Not 'asked.' Commanded me to leave, lock, stock, and barrel, as of June first. And I'm unable to find another rental, even if I were able to pay the outrageous prices they're asking, which I'm not. Unless, of course, you can prevail upon Sundergaard to withdraw his ukase. It seems to me that's the least you can do—as the person responsible for this calamitous turn of events."

"You want me to talk to Sundergaard, is that it?"

"Precisely. As a result of your unauthorized screening

of my video, the local bowdlers have persuaded him to get rid of me, and he's too weak-kneed to stand up to them."

"I'll be happy to talk to him. Is he here?"

"Yes, but I don't know for how long."

"I'll see him first thing tomorrow. But if I were you, I'd drop the idea of suing the county—or me."

With some difficulty Craig rose from the chair. The high color had left his face. "That's up to my lawyer." He slammed the door.

Dave noted Craig had failed to give his lawyer's name. The threatened suit was probably a bluff. Poor old reprobate! And why would Sundergaard, a worldly man, decide suddenly to oust Craig from the cottage he'd inhabited for ten years? If Craig's many liaisons with local young women hadn't earned him Sundergaard's disfavor in the past, why would the showing of a mildly pornographic video do so now?

He phoned Sundergaard at ten the following morning, and arranged to be at Sundergaard's house at eleven.

Going up the long, winding drive, Dave passed Craig's cottage. He caught a brief glimpse of Craig looking out the window and waved.

The simple clapboard cottage was part of the original property Sundergaard had purchased sometime in the 1960s. Sundergaard had hired a famous architect to design the house that now occupied the top of Highfields's highest hill, with a commanding view of the valleys below. Dave had heard that the house's exposed location and glass walls made it impossible to heat in the winter. But Sundergaard was never there in winter, and never more than a few weeks at a time in late spring and early fall.

Sundergaard was waiting for him in the huge living room that filled the entire north wing of the house. Because of the emphasis on horizontal lines in the brown couches and dark paneling, the room seemed low-ceilinged and shadowy, in contrast to the almost blinding light that came through the enveloping window walls.

"I suppose you've come to see me about Mr. Craig," Sundergaard said. His voice held a trace of his Swedish origin.

"Not exactly." Dave sat on one of the long couches. "Who you rent to is none of my business, but I'm curious about what led you to evict Craig now and not years ago. From what I hear, he hasn't always been the ideal tenant."

Sundergaard sucked in his cheeks. The fringe of beard outlining his jaw and his smooth-shaven long upper lip gave him the look of a nineteenth-century Mormon preacher. "I'm not here so much, and at his age he needs a little pleasure." His laugh was surprisingly loud and metallic.

"Then why now? And who told you about the video?"

"I would rather not say." Sundergaard shifted uncomfortably.

"Did someone ask you to keep this matter confidential?"

"Yes. Exactly."

Dave paused to deliberate. He had to frame his questions carefully so they would hold up in court. "Mr. Sundergaard, are you aware that one of the actors in Craig's video was murdered last month?"

"Murdered? My God! I didn't know. I only got here last week. I don't read the local papers."

"It was in *The New York Times*."

"I didn't know the names of the actors Craig used."

"But you do now, don't you?"

"How do you mean?"

"The person who told you about the video must have told you who the actors were. They're all local kids."

167

"Well, as I said, I'm not here so much. The names didn't mean anything to me."

Dave looked at him skeptically. "You don't remember anything about the Durk murder case, where the younger son, Colin Durk, was convicted of killing his father?"

"That happened last year, isn't that so? Is that the murder you're talking about?"

"No. The murder I'm concerned with is the murder of Colin's brother Billy. We're still looking for the killer." There was no point in telling Sundergaard about Colin's confession.

"I see."

"I have reason to believe that the murder was connected in some way to Craig's video. So the information you say you were asked not to reveal may be vital to the solution of the crime."

"I don't see how—" Sundergaard halted in midsentence and fingered his beard. "Well, anything is possible."

"Withholding evidence in a capital crime is itself a crime." Dave smiled, to take the sting from his words.

Sundergaard rose and stood before one of the large windows, his back to Dave. "I would not have agreed to evict poor old Craig if I'd been told it would involve me in a murder case." He turned and eyed Dave. "Lieutenant, if I tell you, you must promise me that you will not call on me to testify—at any time, anywhere."

"I can't promise that. I don't know yet what you'll tell me."

"I can leave here without telling you anything. I have homes in California, Italy, Sweden. What could you do about that? Nothing."

Dave made a quick calculation. He wouldn't be the one to call on Sundergaard to testify. It would be the

State's Attorney. "You've got me there. I won't ask you to testify."

"Fine." Sundergaard sat on a coffee table made from a rough-hewn slab of maple. "Andy McLeod sold me this property twenty-some years ago. He asked me, as a personal favor, to see that Craig left Highfields. Andy said that his granddaughter had been tricked by Craig into appearing in a porno. He was extremely agitated."

"Did he say anything else?"

"Only that he'd cautioned all the county's real-estate agents not to rent to Craig, even if Craig could pay the rents they're asking here. Of course he can't."

"When exactly did Mr. McLeod speak to you?"

"The day after I got back here from the Coast. Last Wednesday. Around noontime."

"Did McLeod say anything about how he'd learned of the video?"

"No."

"But he asked you to keep his visit confidential."

"Yes." Sundergaard gave a crooked smile. "You can see why. It's terrible, some of the things young people get into today, don't you agree?"

"You don't seem to blame Craig."

"My God, no." His metallic laugh cut the air. "Craig's done a lot worse things in his life than make a porno. We all have."

"Still, you gave him his walking papers."

"I can sympathize with Andy. I have granddaughters myself."

"And you say it was last Wednesday he came to you? You're sure about that?"

"Yes. He said he tried to reach me earlier, but I was

still in California and he didn't want to talk about it on the phone."

"Thank you." Dave made for the door. "You've been very helpful."

"You understand, I don't want to get involved."

"Certainly." But you already are, Dave thought.

He needed evidence to establish the date of McLeod's first attempt to reach Sundergaard. It was clear that McLeod had known about the video before it was shown to the MCU staff on Tuesday, although he didn't speak to Sundergaard about it until Wednesday. And Sundergaard might be unavailable or unwilling to repeat in court his statement to Dave that McLeod had tried to reach him earlier. How much earlier?

The phone company didn't keep track of local calls. On the slim chance that McLeod's secretary or McLeod himself might have jotted down Sundergaard's unlisted phone number on an office calendar, Dave drove to McLeod's Maywood office. McLeod was out of the office—showing, in real-estate parlance. McLeod's secretary looked startled when Dave asked to see her boss's desk calendar and hers as well, but she handed them over to him quickly. He failed to find Sundergaard's name or number on either calendar.

Another dead end? If McLeod knew about the video before it arrived in the MCU office, perhaps even before it had been released and shipped by Amphitryon, who had told him? Not his granddaughter, certainly. Not Farnol, who didn't know McLeod and had visited Maywood County only once, as far as Dave could tell. And certainly not Craig, who had every reason to give McLeod a wide berth.

Could it have been Billy? Did Billy approach Sally's

grandfather on April 20 in a final, fatal attempt at extortion? If so, where and when did the meeting take place?

He could confront McLeod and ask him. But if McLeod was the murderer, he wouldn't answer Dave's questions truthfully. They would only serve to alert him. Before questioning Sally's grandfather, Dave needed more to go on than just the fact that McLeod had known about the video at some date prior to its showing in the MCU screening room. He needed some kind of circumstantial evidence. As it stood now, he lacked even the minimum necessary to get a warrant to search Windrush Farm for a Magnum pistol.

He'd have to risk Lucille's anger and ignore his own conviction that infringing a civilian's rights never really paid in the end. But there was no other way to go. His ex-wife might not like it, but he'd do what he had to do.

After leaving word with Phil that he wanted to talk with Harry when Harry came off patrol, he left the barracks. On the way to Maywood High he stopped at Joe's Wagon for a hamburger.

The principal's assistant, a middle-aged woman wearing bright green eye shadow, bustled in her eagerness to oblige him. Dave told her it was vital he see Sally McLeod and Allison Friely without delay. Could she page them, please, and provide him with a private office where he could speak with them?

The assistant immediately put the girls' names on the pager. Then she motioned to a door across the corridor. "You can see them in there. It's empty."

Dave thanked her and stood in the corridor, his hand on the doorknob, waiting for the girls to appear.

They came singly, from opposite ends of the school building. "What are you—?" they asked in unison and exchanged looks of alarm. Dave motioned them into the empty office and closed the door.

He sat on the corner of an old desk. The girls stood uncertainly in the middle of the room. There were no chairs. Besides the desk, there was only an empty metal bookcase.

"I wanted you to be here together. The question I have to ask you is extremely important. Did either of you speak to Mr. McLeod, Sally's grandfather, about the video you made, Sally, with Billy in Florida?"

"No! Not ever!" Sally looked wildly around the room, then turned on Allison, her eyes glazed with panic. "Who? Who told you?"

Allison eyed her coolly. "Billy told me." She shifted her attention to Dave. "No. I never spoke with Mr. McLeod about the video. In fact, I've had no occasion to speak to Sally's grandfather about anything."

Sally began to sob. Softly, between ragged gasps, she asked Dave, "Does Grandpa know? Did you tell him?"

"He does know, Sally, but I didn't tell him, and I'm sure he doesn't hold you responsible." Dave ignored Allison's accusatory gaze. "Do you happen to know where your grandfather keeps his gun?"

Allison put her hand on Sally's wrist. "Don't answer that!" she said sharply. "He's trying to trick you."

Sally's glance wavered. "Grandpa keeps a gun in his bedroom. In the night table."

"You never heard him talk about having another gun?"

"No." She looked at Allison. "Not ever."

"He might have kept a gun in his car. Did you ever happen to look in the glove compartment of his car and see a gun there?"

"No." She eyed him warily. "The glove compartment

in Grandpa's new car locks automatically. I don't know how to open it."

Dave turned to Allison. "Perhaps you saw Mr. McLeod's new car on Route 502 on April twentieth. What kind of car is it?"

"How should I know?"

"It's a Cadillac," Sally said.

"When did your grandfather get this new car?"

"In April. Around income-tax time. Grandpa said he was going to buy it before the government took away all his money."

"What color is it?"

"Brown. With tan leather inside."

Allison half turned her back, as if to disassociate herself from Sally. Dave eased himself off the desk corner and faced her. "Please answer yes or no. Did you see a new brown Cadillac on Route 502 on Friday afternoon, April twentieth?"

Allison lifted her chin. "You're not a lawyer. This isn't a court of law. I don't have to answer you. Besides, even if I'd seen such a car, I wouldn't have known who it belonged to."

"You didn't know Sally's grandfather had bought a new car?"

"No. Why should I?"

Dave maintained a weighted silence. Finally he said, "You saw something on 502 that afternoon that told you who killed Billy Durk. Your pattern of responses to the interrogation in Dr. Esker's office fits such a supposition. I ask you, if you are at all interested in seeing justice prevail, to tell me what that something was."

Allison grabbed Sally's arm. "C'mon, let's get out of here. He's crazy." She pulled Sally toward the door.

He had no right to stop her. "I hope you haven't forgotten what I said about withholding evidence," he said. The feebleness of his parting shot intensified his frustration. To date Allison had defeated him, and not only because he was afraid to press her too hard. Yet he had no doubt she'd seen Billy's murderer that crucial afternoon.

He brooded at his desk. After a month's time none of the shopkeepers or customers along 502 would be able to remember seeing a brand-new brown Cadillac in mid-afternoon of April 20. There was no point in asking Chief Bannerman to do another canvass.

Dave was doodling listlessly on a notepad when Harry walked in. "That bad, huh?" Harry said.

Feeling almost too discouraged to talk, Dave gave Highfields's resident trooper an update on the "Billy Durk murder case," as it was referred to in the press and on TV. But, of course, the press and TV no longer mentioned it. It was old news.

"I see your problem," Harry said. "What do you want me to do?"

"I was thinking maybe I've overlooked something— some kind of lever I could use to open Allison up." He passed his hand over his brow. "We've got to put McLeod at the scene of the crime. And we still have the matter of the gun."

"If McLeod had a Magnum, wouldn't he have bought it here, in the county?" Harry asked.

"There's no gun sale to McLeod in the state records."

"Maybe he bought it before the dealers had to keep records. Fifteen, twenty years ago maybe. Smitty's the only gun dealer in the county that's been in business since the Sixties. No trouble to check."

"Thanks." Harry's suggestion had promise. Dave felt a

shade better. "And you might drop by McLeod's Maywood office. If the Caddy is parked outside, take a close look at it. As close as you can get without breaking the law."

"I get you." Harry grinned. "Cheer up, boss. The troopers always get their man."

"Don't we wish," Dave said.

The news that Lieutenant Littlejohn had appeared at Maywood High and had had a highly secret meeting with Sally McLeod and Allison Friely was known by dinnertime to half the population of Maywood County. But in the homes of Maywood High seniors, the news was of less immediate interest than plans for graduation ceremonies in two weeks. What family members would get tickets? Who would be left at home? Who would feel hurt?

Allison had been named salutatorian. As the result of a C in geometry her first year at Maywood High, her grade-point average was two-tenths of a point below the valedictorian's. She had to compose a speech to deliver at the final class assembly preceding the graduation ceremonies.

Immediately after supper Allison went up to her room to work on the speech. At the bottom of the stairwell the phone rang. Annemarie picked up the receiver.

"Isn't it simply outrageous," Rose McLeod said, "a policeman coming to the school? Are they allowed to do that? Treating Allison and Sally like criminals! Don't you think we should make some kind of protest?"

It was the first Annemarie had heard of it. "Allison didn't tell me," she said. "Do you mean one of the troopers came to Maywood High to see Sally and Allison?"

"Yes. Lieutenant Littlejohn. He's been to the house to question Sally and Andy and me about Billy's murder, but I think he's got terrible nerve to go to school and get them out of class like that and put them in a little room and give them the third degree." She sounded breathless. "Can't we do something to protect our girls from this sort of harassment?"

"What does your husband say?"

"Oh, you know Andy. He said the lieutenant was just doing his job and it's not worth making a fuss. So close to graduation, too."

"Maybe he's right. I don't think it bothered Allison, or she would have told me."

"Sally was awfully upset, but I know I worry about her too much. You know, every once in a while I catch her in tears—over that terrible boy."

"Give her time," Annemarie said. "It's only been a month."

"It seems longer than that, doesn't it?" Rose McLeod sighed. "Well, I thought I'd see how you felt. Allison is so level-headed, isn't she?"

After she cradled the phone, Annemarie debated about going up to Allison's room and asking her about the incident. She decided against it. Allison wouldn't like her work on her speech interrupted.

Lucille heard about it from Doreen Wednesday morning. In the few minutes before her first patient of the day arrived, she phoned the barracks.

"I heard you questioned Allison again—yesterday, at school. I thought you understood me Sunday. Allison is not well, although she's extremely skilled in hiding her distress. Any further stress could easily push her over the edge. If anything happens to her, I'll hold you responsible."

"Lay off me, will you? Unless you've got something more to contribute than psychobabble."

His irritated tone told her more than his words. "You didn't get her to talk, did you?"

"She didn't give me an inch, if that's what you want to know. Satisfied?"

"Dave, stop treating me like an adversary. I'd like very much to see you clear Colin and solve Billy's murder."

"You would, would you? Well, Doctor, as far as I'm concerned, it's solved. But without your patient's testimony, I can't get the murderer arrested for speeding."

"You know who did it?"

"Yes."

"And it's not Allison, is it?"

"No."

She knew he'd refuse to give her the murderer's identity. Besides, by a process of elimination, she was almost certain she'd identified the killer on her own. "You can't indict on Allison's testimony alone. Once you've got other proof, I'm sure she'll come forward."

"Thanks, Doctor, for your vote of confidence."

Dave's sour sarcasm set the tone for the day. Allison failed to appear at three-thirty. When four o'clock came and there was still no word from her, Lucille called her home.

"She's not here," Annemarie said. "You're sure she didn't call your office? She might have had something to do at school because of the graduation."

"I'll call the school. And if she comes home, please let me know immediately."

Lucille phoned the school and was transferred to the teacher in charge of the pre-graduation assembly program. No, Allison wasn't there. Her first speech rehearsal was scheduled for Friday morning.

Lucille phoned the McLeods', on the chance that Allison might be with Sally.

"I didn't see Allison all day today," Sally said.

"Was she very upset after your meeting yesterday with Lieutenant Littlejohn?"

"I was a lot more shook up than she was. The lieutenant said Grandpa knew something I didn't want him to know."

"I'm terribly worried about Allison. She missed her appointment this afternoon. If you hear from her, please call me immediately. I'll be here at the clinic for another hour, and after that I'll be home." She gave Sally the two phone numbers.

"Why did Billy have to die?" Sally asked. "What did he do that was so terrible he had to die? Do you know, Dr. Esker?"

"I'm sorry, Sally. I don't." She was anxious to terminate the conversation. "Please, please call the moment you hear."

She next called the barracks. Dave wasn't there. Sergeant Hillis took the phone.

"You mean she didn't show for her appointment?" he said. "Hell, it's a nice day. She's probably riding around with her friends. She's a senior, isn't she? All the seniors get itchy feet around graduation time. I've known some of them start with a shopping spree on 502 and end with a camping weekend in Vermont. Don't worry, you'll hear from her soon."

Lucille tried Dave's apartment. No answer.

Doreen left for the day. Lucille waited by her office phone another fifteen minutes, then drove home, breaking the speed limit all the way. What if someone tried to get her while she was en route?

The silence in her house was deafening. She called Allison's home again.

"No, I haven't heard from her," Annemarie said. "But it isn't six o'clock yet. I'm sure she'll be home for supper."

She wasn't. Lucille phoned Constable Burns and asked him to search the Highfields roads for Allison's dark green Mustang. "She's a troubled girl," she explained. "She may have harmed herself. Please don't wait to look for her, please."

When Lucille hadn't heard from the constable by eight, she again phoned Allison's home.

"Stop calling us," Annemarie said, her voice thin and shrill. "She was a fine, normal, intelligent girl, and now"— her voice broke—"now, for all I know, she's lying somewhere in the mud—like Billy was."

That Annemarie, who had brought Allison to her, should now accuse her of causing Allison's depression, was not at all unusual. Parents, especially those who felt guilty, often began to blame Lucille for their child's problems at some point in the therapy.

"Please, I'm just as worried about her as you—"

"Get off the phone!" Annemarie slammed the receiver.

At ten o'clock Lucille finally found Dave at home. He'd been out questioning the three witnesses who had seen Allison's green Mustang on Route 502 on April 20. Had they happened to notice a brand-new brown Cadillac on the highway at the same time they'd seen Allison's car? Not one of them could remember seeing such a car.

On his way back to his apartment, he'd heard about Allison on the police radio. "Didn't they tell you?" he asked Lucille. "Allison walked in her front door half an hour ago. She was sitting in her car off West Road, thinking things over."

Lucille felt the tightness around her heart suddenly

relax. "Her mother was very upset," she said shakily. "I hope this doesn't mean she'll stop Allison's therapy."

"I wouldn't worry. When this is all over, you'll get your patient back."

"When this is all over. When will that be?"

"Soon, I hope."

"In time to save Colin?"

"Maybe. Maybe not." Dave paused. She heard him breathing heavily. "Anyway, your sick cookie is safe home in bed. And if she's willing to see Colin fry, there's nothing I can do about it."

She was too drained by anxiety to respond to his needling. "I guess not," she said.

CHAPTER

Thursday morning Dave reran the tape of Allison's interrogation in Lucille's office. He was especially puzzled by her answer when he asked her if she'd seen anyone following Billy. She'd said, "I did not see any person following Billy." Why had she answered his question in such an odd way? And if she hadn't seen "any person," what then had she seen? A car? But he tended to believe her when she'd said on Tuesday, in the Maywood High School office, that she didn't know Andy McLeod had a new car. If it was someone else's car, whose could it have been? Whatever it was she had seen on Route 502 that Friday afternoon, he was positive it had enabled her to identify Billy's killer.

Harry came in shortly before noon.

"Those MCU bastards!" Harry clenched his fists.

"Easy! Easy!" Dave motioned him to sit. "What happened?"

"MCU took all Smitty's records. I hightailed it over to the MCU office, and guess what? They won't let me see them. They have to get a special clerk to look them over for me—a documents custodian, somebody who knows how to read records, right? I'm illiterate, right? Anyway, no record of any sale of any kind of gun to Andrew McLeod. The whole damn morning wasted."

"Maybe not." Dave paused, then continued, "We've got a name now, which we didn't have before. Go over to the Maywood Gun Club and find out if McLeod was ever a member. Ask about that dentist the Hallberg kid said owned a Magnum. Find out the dentist's name and find out what dentist McLeod goes to. If they're one and the same, I'll take it from there."

Harry nodded and made notes.

"Did you get a chance to stop by McLeod's Maywood office? Was the Caddy there?"

"Yup, but locked tight. I figured it had one of those alarm systems, so I'd better not mess with it. Besides, if I got inside and found something, I would have tainted the evidence."

"Good judgment." Without question, Harry was the best rookie Troop B had had in years. "What's his license number?"

"It's one of those vanity plates. AM one. 'Andy McLeod number one.' The old guy is pretty stuck on himself."

"That's it!" Why hadn't he thought of it before? "That's what Allison saw on 502—the license plate. That's how she knew it was Andy McLeod." Could he get her to admit it? "Christ! We've got to find another witness."

Harry nodded sympathetically as he left.

Dave called Santini at MCU headquarters.

"Are you still working on the Durk Case?"

"Sure. The S.A. wants more evidence. For a change."

"Who's defending Colin?"

"So far only Rubin, the Conyac lawyer. It'll probably be Legal Aid when it comes to trial."

"Not if I can help it it won't," Dave said.

"I thought that was your wife's ticket—helping the poor oppressed criminal and to hell with the victim."

Dave ignored the barb. "One of your people gave one of my troopers the runaround this morning, and I'd like to know—are we working together on this or aren't we?"

"I don't know of anything we've dug up that we haven't told you about," Santini said.

"You took the records from Smitty's Gun Shop and I don't recall hearing word one about that."

"They didn't tell us anything, that's why. If they'd given us a lead, we would have told you. We'd still like to find the murder weapon. In a month a two-time murderer comes to trial and if we don't give the S.A. a better case, in October he could march right out of Conyac and we couldn't touch him."

"You're not looking for anybody else as the killer?"

"Hell no. We've got the confession. Why? You got somebody?"

"Maybe," Dave said. "Maybe not."

"I expect you'll let us know when you're ready."

"I expect I will."

Dave buried himself in administrative work for most of the afternoon. He and Sergeant Hillis had to make out the duty roster for the second half of the year, always a difficult assignment. It was impossible not to show some favoritism, but he tried to keep it to a minimum.

Harry phoned in shortly before five. "I had trouble locating the guy who runs the gun club. It's only open nights and weekends. The manager was nice enough, though. He opened the office and looked in the old files.

Andrew McLeod was a member of the Maywood Gun Club from 1947 to 1964. He won some prizes, too."

"What about the dentist?"

"Dr. Michaels. I called his office. He's been McLeod's dentist for the last twenty years. McLeod still has some of his own teeth—at eighty-one years old. Pretty good, huh?"

"Thanks, Harry. I'll see you tomorrow."

He hung up and asked Phil to get Dr. Michaels's office before he left. Dave spoke to the dentist's receptionist. "I'd like to see Dr. Michaels as soon as possible," he said.

"The doctor is with a patient. May I ask what the problem is?"

"It's an emergency. But it's not a toothache. It's a police matter."

"Oh! Well, just a minute. I'll speak to Dr. Michaels." She was back on the phone in two minutes. "Dr. Michaels will be happy to see you in his office at six. Is that agreeable?"

"Yes, fine. I'll be there."

At about the same time Dave was driving along Highfields Road to Maywood, Lucille was taking her purse out of her desk, preparing to leave for the day. On looking up she was startled to see Allison standing in the doorway.

"I'm sorry about yesterday. I really am." She sounded breathless.

"Did your mother tell you to come here and apologize?"

Allison shook her head. "She's boiling mad."

"That's understandable." There was no point in burdening Allison with recriminations. "Come on in. I don't have any pressing reason to leave right now." She put her purse back in the desk drawer. "Annemarie doesn't know you're here?"

184

Allison sat on the edge of the couch, her knees pressed together. "No. She thinks I'm at school."

"You'd better be home pretty quick then."

Allison smiled her American Beauty smile. "You're right."

"Do you feel like everything is falling in on you all at once—your speech and graduation and Lieutenant Littlejohn?"

"A little." Allison looked down. "He knows who did it, doesn't he?"

Lucille nodded. "How long have you known?"

"Since they found Billy's body."

"You saw him following Billy?"

"I didn't recognize the car, but I saw the license plate."

"You'll eventually have to tell the police."

"I can't." Allison's fingers twisted. "I just can't. He's an old man. He looks healthy, but he has cancer. They should leave him alone and let nature take its course."

"That wouldn't satisfy society's need for vengeance."

"Vengeance?" Allison grimaced. "For killing Billy? Society ought to give him a medal."

"Murder is wrong."

"Not always."

"It's an old problem." Lucille eyed Allison with sympathy. "I'm glad you decided to tell me. I was afraid you thought I had something to do with Dave coming to Maywood High, and you no longer trusted me."

"I didn't for awhile. Then I thought it over."

"Last night—while half the county police were looking for you." Lucille smiled at Allison as they walked toward the door. "I'll see you next Wednesday, as usual?"

"Yes. And thanks for not being angry about yesterday."

Dave arrived in Dr. Michaels's office a few minutes before six and had to wait for the dentist to finish with his last patient.

Dr. Michaels was short, round-faced, and bald. He guided Dave into his office. "What's this all about?"

"We're trying to find a missing gun."

The dentist gave him a shrewd look. "Anything to do with the murder of that kid on the Conyac farm?"

"Possibly."

"I don't see how I can help you."

"I understand you own a Magnum .357. Has it ever been out of your possession?"

"Definitely not. I keep it locked in a gun cabinet."

"You have a lot of guns then?"

"I've got a"—the dentist pursed his lips—"sort of a collection. A few old rifles, shotguns, a couple of pistols."

"Have you ever sold any of your collection?"

"Sure. When I have duplicates."

"Was one of the duplicates you sold a Magnum .357?"

The dentist put a finger to his forehead. "Let's see. It was some time ago—maybe fifteen years?" He looked at Dave as if he expected Dave to freshen his memory. "Yes, fifteen or sixteen years ago. That's when I bought the Magnum I have now, the one they all kid me about."

"Who did you sell the old Magnum to?"

"That's easy. Andy McLeod. Eighty-one and he still has most of his own teeth. Thanks to good genes, healthy living, and me."

"You don't happen to have a receipt for that sale, do you?"

"After fifteen years? I doubt it."

"I'd appreciate it if you'd look for it."

Dr. Michaels looked amused. "What's old Andy got himself into? You think his gun was used—"

"I can't say. I hope you'll keep my visit confidential." Dave extended his hand. "If you find the receipt, you can reach me at the barracks."

He drove the patrol car back to the barracks and got in his own car for the short drive to his apartment. He wanted to savor over a bottle of beer the good feeling he had. Not quite all the pieces were in hand yet, but he was getting close.

Would McLeod's gun test positive as the murder weapon? Besides the Durk gun, which Ballistics had ruled out, it was the only Magnum in Maywood County that could be linked to Billy's murder.

The big question was: Did McLeod still have the gun, and if he did, could Dave get possession of it without alerting McLeod? If McLeod found out he was under suspicion—Allison or his granddaughter or even Dr. Michaels might tell him—he'd get rid of the gun if he hadn't got rid of it already. And then they'd be back to square one.

Dave was torn. If he acted precipitously, he could blow it. If he waited, he could lose the whole ball game.

Throughout his career in law enforcement he'd been guided by the principle: When in doubt, don't. The passage of time often made difficult decisions simpler or, sometimes, unnecessary.

If the gun was gone, it was gone—and they might never find it. If the gun was still in McLeod's possession, it would probably stay there, even if McLeod learned he was under suspicion.

Dave's equanimity vanished when the phone rang and Garrison Craig's voice blasted from the receiver. "What the fuck are you trying to do to me?" he roared.

"Hold on," Dave said. "What happened?"

"Those storm troopers over in Morgantown had at me with the rubber hoses all the fucking afternoon, that's what. What the hell did you tell them? It's bad enough you confiscated my property and left me without a roof over my head, but—"

"I didn't have anything to do with that. It was Andy McLeod who asked Sundergaard to—"

"Who the fuck cares who it was. I want to know what you told those Nazis in Morgantown."

"You mean the Major Crime Unit detectives? I don't recall telling them anything. They saw your name in the credits of your—quote—educational video."

"They seem to think I had something to do with Billy Durk's murder. Who gave them that idea if it wasn't you?"

"Just seeing Billy in the video might have given them the idea. Billy tried to extort money from the Farnols and from Ellis Somers. My guess is that the MCU detectives wanted to find out if he tried it on you."

"Christ, everybody in the county knows I don't have a pot to pee in."

"Maybe not MCU."

"I'm not going to roll over and let you stomp on me. You'll hear from my lawyer."

"I'm sorry you feel that way."

"You'll be sorry all right!"

Despite the crash from Craig's end of the line, Dave put down the receiver slowly. Craig's abusive language could mean he was hiding something. But what? Craig hadn't reacted one way or another to Dave's mention of Andy McLeod.

Should he tell Santini about McLeod's Magnum? If he did, MCU would go after the gun without delay. And if it turned out to be the murder weapon, MCU would take credit for finding it. That's the way the game was played.

No, he wouldn't tell MCU. And he wouldn't go to McLeod until he had a witness to McLeod's presence on Route 502 the afternoon of the murder, a witness who, unlike Allison Friely, would be willing to talk. Did such a creature exist—anywhere?

That night he dreamed he saw a gleaming brown Caddy in the middle of a cornfield, the tall, dark green cornstalks almost obscuring the car. The dream was stranger than the few Technicolor dreams he'd had in the past because the figure crouching between the rows of corn was totally without color, a black unidentifiable shape.

The next day Harry came in during the morning break.

"I almost called you at home last night to find out," Harry said. "What did the dentist say?"

"He sold McLeod a Magnum about fifteen years ago."

"Heh, wow! We've got him."

"Easy, easy. Even if it's the murder weapon, we still haven't placed him at the scene of the crime. Someone else might have used the gun."

"Damn!" Harry sat and scratched his head. "You talked to the witnesses who saw that girl Allison, right?"

Dave nodded.

"Wasn't there someone else? Didn't Bannerman say—" Suddenly Harry leapt up. "Heh! The lady who was interested in commercial property. She said she saw a big shiny new car parked on the shoulder right next to the logging road. You remember?"

"I love you," Dave said. He dialed the Maywood police station and asked the policeman who answered the phone to get him the name and address of the woman who reported a car parked near the logging road. In a few minutes the policeman called back. "Mrs. Harriet Doran. She lives on Maple Lane in North Maywood."

"Thanks." Dave asked Phil to look up her number and get her on the phone.

Luck was with him—she was at home.

"Mrs. Doran," Dave said, "I'm interested in the car you told Chief Bannerman you saw on Route 502 the afternoon of April twentieth. Would you have a few minutes to spare this morning to help us identify that car?"

"If you come right over. I've got a doctor's appointment at eleven."

"I'll be there in fifteen minutes."

Dave turned to Harry. "See how fast you can find McLeod's car. Then call me on the radio and I'll bring the lady over."

Harry rushed out the door. He burned rubber getting the patrol car out of the barracks parking lot.

Dave drove at moderate speed to North Maywood. Mrs. Doran lived at the end of a dead-end street in one of the newer developments. Just as he turned into her driveway, the car radio crackled.

"The Caddy is parked outside McLeod's Maywood office," Harry said. "I'll keep an eye on it."

"Be right there." Dave rang Mrs. Doran's doorbell. When she opened the door, her handbag was over her arm.

"You're the policeman who called me?" she asked.

Dave showed her his identification.

"Then let's go." She gave him a pleasant smile as she entered the patrol car.

As Dave neared McLeod's office, he noticed Harry's patrol car across the highway. Parked on the cement apron that stretched from the front to the back of the real-estate office were four cars—a VW Rabbit, a Ford Escort station wagon, the brown Caddy, and a silver-gray Mercedes with a New York license plate.

"That's the car," Mrs. Doran said, pointing to the Caddy.

"You're sure?"

"Yes. That is definitely the car I saw."

"You were on your way home?"

"I'd finished shopping. It was the middle of the afternoon. I don't know the exact time, but I'd guess it was about three-thirty."

"Did you see anyone get into or out of the car?"

"No." She gave him a sympathetic look. "Have I helped any?"

"A great deal." Some civilians were a joy to do business with. "Let's get you home in time for your appointment."

He made a U-turn and sped toward North Maywood. At her door he said, "We may have to call on you to testify at some future date."

"I'll be glad to testify," she said.

Halfway back down 502 Harry came on the radio. "Was it?" he asked.

"That's the car," Dave said.

A few minutes later Harry reported, "McLeod and a man just got in the Caddy and headed toward Highfields. I'm following him."

Dave put on the siren and stepped on the accelerator until he was within sight of Harry's car. "Do you recognize who's with him?" Dave asked.

"No. Might be a customer."

"You pull up ahead of him and I'll stay back."

He saw Harry pull out into the passing lane and then lost sight of him. A few minutes later Harry announced: "Left on West Road. I almost missed him."

Dave turned onto West Road and saw Harry's car parked about a hundred feet in from the intersection with Highfields Road. He parked his car behind Harry's and got out. Harry pointed down West Road. "They stopped at the Durk place."

"Maybe Mrs. Durk is going to sell. She hasn't got more than six acres left, but if anybody can get a good price for her, it's Andy."

"Should we wait?"

Dave nodded. "When he's finished with the customer he has to come back this way. There's nothing to sell beyond the Durk place. Grunewald's going to keep farming till the day he dies."

"McLeod has some nerve," Harry said. "Kills the woman's boy, then goes and sells her land."

"That's the business he's in. Besides, we don't know positively that he killed Billy Durk, and we're only guessing that the man with him is out looking for property."

Fifteen minutes went by before they heard the engine noise of a car straining up the steep hill from the Durk house. They got their patrol cars on the road before the Caddy appeared at the top of the rise.

Approaching the intersection with Highfields Road, Dave said, "You turn left, I'll turn right. Whoever loses goes back to the barracks."

"Gotcha."

Dave saw the Caddy in his rear-view mirror. He cruised east on Highfields Road and Route 502 for two miles, then pulled into a gas station, letting the Caddy pass him. Just as the car was out of sight around a curve in 502, he pulled out. He narrowed the gap and saw the Caddy turn left and stop on the narrow apron in front of McLeod's office. McLeod and his customer stepped out of the car and exchanged a few words. They shook hands and the customer climbed into the Mercedes and drove away. McLeod remained standing in front of his office. He pointed to Dave's car stopped on the shoulder across the highway and motioned him to cross over. Dave made a quick U-turn across four lanes of highway and parked next to the Caddy.

"Did you want to see me?" McLeod asked. His eyes crinkled as if Dave amused him.

"Yes. Actually I'd like to see your gun. Do you keep it in your car?"

McLeod opened the passenger door of the Caddy and unlocked the glove compartment. He took out a black pistol with a distinctive long barrel. "Is this what you're looking for?" he said.

"Ballistics will have to test it."

"How long will that take?"

"A couple of days."

"I see." McLeod's look of detached amusement remained. "Shouldn't you give me some kind of receipt for the gun?"

Dave nodded. He pulled out his notepad and quickly scribbled a receipt.

"You ought to make a note that I handed it over to you voluntarily, without coercion." The amused twinkle was more pronounced.

"I'll testify to that effect," Dave said.

"If it comes to that." For a moment McLeod's shoulders sagged and he looked his eighty-one years. But he straightened himself quickly. "However, I don't think it will," he added.

Beads of sweat dotted his high freckled forehead. A spasm seemed to course through him and his jaw tightened.

"Would you like to make a statement?" Dave said.

"I'll have to think about it." McLeod half turned away,

then turned back. "It will depend on what Ballistics says." His old man's voice was steady and strong. He waved at Dave cheerfully as he entered his office.

Dave was puzzled by McLeod's reaction. The old man was knowledgeable about guns. He might know that Ballistics wouldn't tag his gun as the murder weapon unless the groovings on the fatal bullet matched those on another bullet fired from the same gun. But the bullet that killed Billy had been distorted by lodging in Billy's skull. Perhaps that's what he was counting on.

Dave drove to Morgantown and gave the gun to Doc Prentiss at the Ballistics lab. "I won't be responsible for what happens to you if anybody besides myself gets your report," he threatened. "That means the press, MCU, anybody." Scowling, he headed back to the barracks. Doc wouldn't have the report till the following Wednesday because Monday was Memorial Day. The whole goddamn weekend to wait and hope nothing leaked out. Or McLeod didn't do something irreversible to cheat justice.

The weather made the wait worse. If it had been just a drizzle, he would still have been able to play golf, but it poured, steadily, all Saturday and Sunday. The heavy downpour turned the plowed fields to mud once again. Small new green leaves on the trees glistened white against the sooty skies.

He tried to distract himself by catching up with some long-delayed household chores. But by Sunday afternoon there was nothing left to do. Swallowing his resentment over the way she'd acted the previous Sunday, he phoned Lucille.

"I need a little psychological first-aid," he said. Lucille called it his Florence Nightingale gambit. It didn't always work.

"It *is* a depressing day, isn't it," she said. She sounded

friendly enough. "I'm still twanging from the scare Allison gave all of us Wednesday. She came in Thursday and apologized."

"I thought a couple of drinks and dinner would improve the internal weather."

"Is that an invitation?"

"What did you think it was? A weather report?" Her laughter had a warm, comforting sound. "Okay if I pick you up in an hour? Give you time to get the rollers out of your hair."

"I don't use rollers and you know it."

While he showered and changed into something more respectable, he envisioned Lucille's long brown hair, fanned out on the pillow beside him. Maybe he'd never get over her, never find someone else, unless he moved away, do what he'd long ago told her he wanted to do—find a big-city administrative job, insulated from day-to-day contact with petty crooks and grifters and foul-mouthed civilians. But he couldn't do that until he got his Ph.D. And here it was, almost time to sign up for summer classes. Should he take Advanced Russian? Something else? He'd been so busy with the Durk case, he hadn't had time to look over the summer catalog. And when would he find time to work on a dissertation? He was back inside a vicious circle. He couldn't get out of the rut he was in unless he got out of the rut he was in.

Actually, his present job hadn't bored him in the past month. And the fact that the Billy Durk murder case was near solution made him feel pretty good. In a big-city job, he doubted he'd ever feel that kind of satisfaction.

Lucille looked especially lovely in a blue silk shirt. She wore a fluffy white sweater over her shoulders.

"The Peaceable Kingdom okay?" he asked.

"Fine. With all this rain the brook must be up to its banks again."

"About where it was last month," Dave said, "before—"

"Before Billy was murdered."

"I won't talk business tonight if you don't," he said.

And they didn't. The evening was completed with a movie. The movie was good and provided the distraction they both needed.

Memorial Day was a work day for most of the troopers. Dave spent the day at the barracks. In each little town in the county only a handful of spectators, huddled under umbrellas, watched the parades.

By Tuesday afternoon, Dave couldn't restrain his curiosity. He phoned Ballistics on the slim chance Doc would have the report ready ahead of time. But Doc said, "We're just getting to it now. Try me tomorrow afternoon."

When he phoned Wednesday, Doc said, "It's unofficial, but it looks like you've found the murder weapon."

"Is the match good enough to stand up in court?" Dave asked.

"You know better than to ask that," Doc said. "You'll get the official report by Friday and you can take it from there."

Doc's unwillingness to promise his finding was unassailable was typical. He rarely claimed 100 percent certainty, but if he reported 90 percent certainty, that was enough.

Dave phoned McLeod's Maywood office. McLeod wasn't there, but was expected. Dave gave McLeod's secretary the barracks phone number. "Please have him call me as soon as he comes in," he said.

While he waited he thought about attitudes. The kind of respectful treatment he accorded McLeod contrasted sharply with the kind of treatment the ordinary criminal received. Even a petty shoplifter got rougher handling than Dave was giving Andrew McLeod, a murderer. Why? Because he was rich? Because he was old? Because Dave lacked sympathy for the victim?

The phone rang.

"Your gun matches the murder bullet," he told McLeod. "Are you prepared to give us a statement?"

"Yes, but I'll have to speak to a lawyer, and I'd like him to be present when I make my statement. Would tomorrow at eleven be convenient?"

It was as if he was making an appointment to show property, not confess to murder. "Eleven tomorrow will be fine," Dave said.

At ten-thirty Thursday, Sergeant Hillis came in to Dave's office in order to witness the statement.

On the dot of eleven the brown Caddy entered the barracks parking area. Dave recognized the passenger as Glen Fitzmaurice, the county's top criminal lawyer. Fitzmaurice led the way into Dave's office and shook hands with Dave and Hillis. "I assume we all know why I'm here," he said.

McLeod smiled. He looked totally relaxed.

Hillis tested the recorder, then read McLeod his rights.

McLeod nodded and cleared his throat. "I'd like to give a little background first, if you don't mind," he began. "My granddaughter Sally became infatuated with Billy Durk several months ago. I understand that she wasn't alone in her infatuation. He affected many of the young girls at Maywood High in the same way. But he was able to convince Sally that she was the only girl he cared for. When he came to the house, I frankly didn't like what I saw. He was brash and impudent, and at the same time there was something secretive about him, something devious and unpleasant. I thought Sally would eventually see what an unappealing fellow he was. Her infatuation would burn itself out."

McLeod paused. His eyes moved from Fitzmaurice to Dave to Hillis. "Of course, I was wrong. During the spring break, without my approval, she went with him to Florida. Mrs. McLeod and I were understandably upset, and when she failed to return by the end of spring break, we were beside ourselves with worry. I asked Lieutenant Littlejohn to phone the police in Key Doro. He did and reported that the Farnols, the people who had invited Billy and Sally to visit them, were respectable, responsible people. Then Sally phoned and said she and Billy were returning on the Farnols' private plane. When Sally arrived home, I was naturally very relieved."

He took a handkerchief from his pocket and wiped his brow. Fitzmaurice gave him a worried look. "I tried to keep out of the way when Billy came to the house. I found his manner extremely abrasive and I try to keep my blood pressure down." He gave a wry smile. "I still thought Sally's infatuation would disappear in time."

He closed his eyes and took a deep breath. "That brings us to April twentieth. At around three in the afternoon I was on my way back to my Maywood office after showing the Davis place in Highfields Landing to Mr. and Mrs. Olin of Binghamton, New York. I saw Billy Durk's new motorcycle parked in front of my Highfields office. Knowing that he was bothering Sally while she was at work made me angry, very angry. I was beginning to fear that my granddaughter wouldn't wake up until it was too late. I pulled into a space in back of the Highfields office and waited for Billy to come out. I caught him just as he was about to climb on his motorcycle and asked him to take a seat in my car. As he sat down in the back seat he said, 'I'm going to have a car like this one of these days, just you wait and see.' I said to him, 'Not on Sally's money, you won't.' And then I said, 'I want you to stop seeing Sally. I'm prepared to give you one thousand dollars if you tell her you've fallen in love with someone else and can't see her anymore.'"

McLeod's skin had taken on a grayish cast. His words came more and more slowly. "Billy laughed. 'You'll pay me a lot more than a thousand dollars,' he said, 'and I won't stop seeing Sally, either.' I didn't know what to say to that, so I kept quiet. Then he said, with this vicious smirk on his face, 'When Sally and me were in Florida, we made a dirty movie. We're both in it. You want to keep it from being shown, you're going to have to give me four thousand dollars right now and no bullshit'—that's his language."

McLeod looked at Dave questioningly. "Could I have a glass of water, please?" Dave rang Phil to bring in the water. After McLeod had taken a few gulps, he put the glass aside. "I said to Billy, 'Get out of here this minute.' He got out of the car. He said, 'You better get me the four grand by tomorrow, Grandpa.' He was laughing when he got on his motorcycle and turned left on 502, going toward Maywood. I decided to follow him. He must have seen me in his side mirror and thought I was trying to catch up with him to pay him. He slowed down just as he came near the Conyac farm and turned right into the old logging road. I pulled over onto the shoulder and took my gun out of the glove compartment. It's an old gun, but it's in top condition even though it's years since I've used it. And my eyes are still good at a distance.

"I walked along the logging road, some fifty feet in from the highway. The mud in the road was six inches deep from all the rain. About halfway along the trail there's a straight section where the road widens out a bit. I saw Billy

up ahead, some thirty feet away, leaning over his motorcycle. I don't think he heard me, though I wasn't trying to
creep up on him. I took aim and fired. One shot, that's all.
He staggered forward into the woods. I didn't check to see
if he was dead. I went back out the logging road, got in my
car, wiped off the gun with a rag I keep in the glove compartment, put the gun in, and drove the rest of the way to
my Maywood office. I finished the day's work and went
home at the usual hour. I want you to know that I haven't
once felt sorry for what I did, but I *was* sorry that Colin
was under suspicion. I planned to come forward if it looked
like you were about to bring him to trial. And you'll find a
full confession attached to my will in my safe-deposit box. I
hoped I'd be dead before you tagged me as the murderer.
That way there wouldn't have been much notice paid in the
newspapers and TV and my wife and granddaughter would
have been left in peace." A spasm shook McLeod's body.
His chin lifted with a jerk and his eyes closed.

Dave, with a nod from Fitzmaurice, signed off the
tape. Fitzmaurice gently patted his client's shoulder, then
asked Dave, "Could I have a word with you? Privately?"

Dave told Hillis to keep an eye on McLeod and led
the lawyer to a vacant office.

"My client is a dying man," Fitzmaurice said. "I'm not
going to dispute McLeod's statement at this point, but
eventually I may have to. I'll do whatever is necessary to
keep my client from coming to trial."

"I understand," Dave said.

Allison's salutatory address before the graduating class of
Maywood High School won unanimous praise. In her first
session with Lucille following graduation, she said, "I really
don't think the speech was all that good. People were just
being nice."

"At any rate," Lucille said, "that's an improvement on people being hypocrites."

"I did say that once, didn't I?" Allison's grin was sly. "Well then, let's say people were being hypocritically nice. I don't want to contradict myself."

The session went well. Allison appeared, for perhaps the first time, to want to cooperate fully in the therapy. Before leaving the office she said, "When are you going on vacation?"

Lucille reflected for a moment. "I thought I'd take a late vacation this year. The middle of September on the Cape is my favorite time. You'll be off to Wisconsin by then."

"We hope," Allison said.

Andy McLeod died on Friday, October 19, exactly six months from the day he shot and killed Billy Durk. The case never came before a judge and jury.

Lucille looked at Dave in the candlelight that illuminated their tiny round table at their favorite Italian restaurant in Danbury. She smiled at him over her glass of red wine. "What was the very first moment you knew?"

"When Sundergaard said it was McLeod who asked him to get rid of Craig. Everything fell into place."

"And not before? You didn't have McLeod on your list of suspects?"

"His alibi checked out, so there was no way to put him on the scene. Besides, you don't think of eighty-one-year-old grandfathers as murder suspects, somehow."

"There's a chance, then, that you might never have solved the crime." She looked at him slyly. "He wanted to be caught."

"I don't know about that. He said in his statement that he would have come forward if it looked like we were going to bring Colin to trial. And he had a written confession attached to his will."

"If he'd got rid of the gun, the state would have had trouble proving he was guilty." She nodded. "Yes, he wanted to be caught."

"He knew he was dying."

"That, too." She paused. "He got Mae Durk to invest the money from selling the house, so the income is enough for her and Colin to live on. But Mavis told me Colin is barely scraping by. His heart is in farming, not in schoolwork. I shiver whenever I think about him seeing his brother lying dead in the woods and living with that knowledge the entire week you were searching for Billy, without saying a word to anyone."

Dave frowned. "After so much tragedy, I figured the Durks would leave the county, live somewhere else."

"This is where their roots are. They found a small house to rent in North Maywood." She smiled. "Nobody ever wants to leave Maywood County, you know that."

Dave answered her smile with a grin. "Not even old rascal Craig. He's back in Sundergaard's cottage. With a new girlfriend." Dave shook his head. "Maybe I'll do my dissertation on the elderly criminal."

"That's not such a bad idea."

"You hear from Allison?"

"A short letter last week—one page. She says she's too busy at the university even to feel homesick. And she may have fallen in love. She sounds fine."

Dave held his glass of wine in the air and they clicked glasses. "We're not so bad at our jobs, are we?"

"Not bad at all," Lucille said.